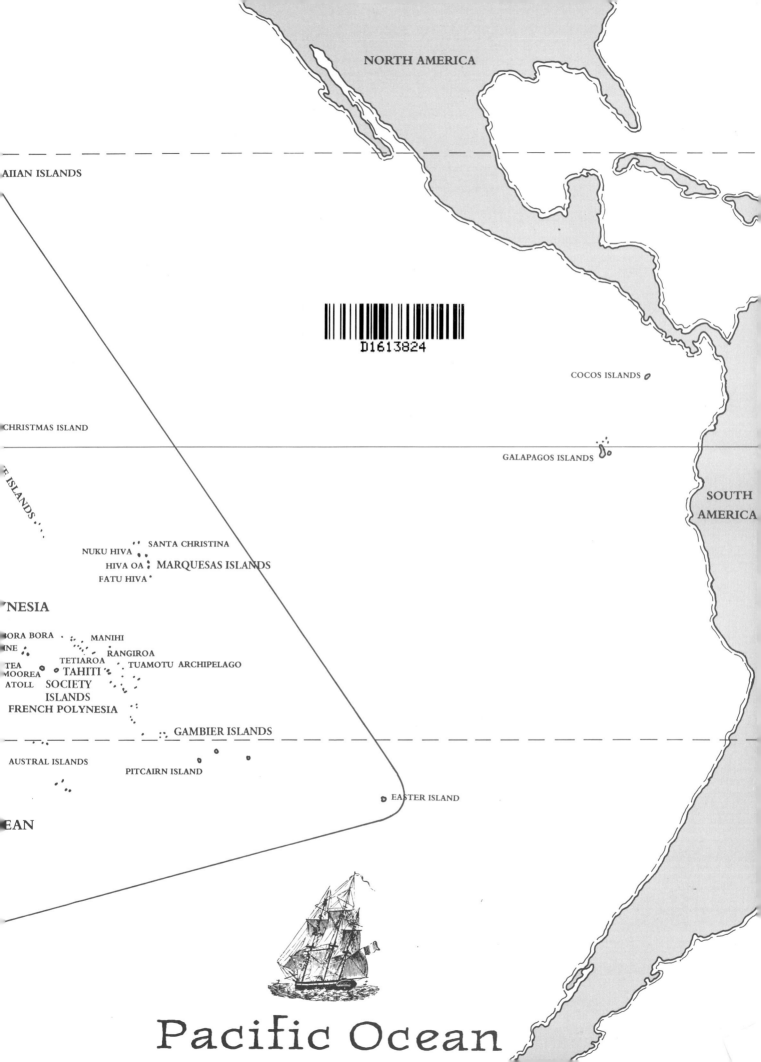

NORTH AMERICA

AIIAN ISLANDS

D1613824

COCOS ISLANDS

CHRISTMAS ISLAND

GALAPAGOS ISLANDS

SOUTH
AMERICA

E ISLANDS

SANTA CHRISTINA
NUKU HIVA
HIVA OA MARQUESAS ISLANDS
FATU HIVA

NESIA

BORA BORA MANIHI
NE
RANGIROA
TEA TETIAROA TUAMOTU ARCHIPELAGO
MOOREA TAHITI
ATOLL SOCIETY
ISLANDS
FRENCH POLYNESIA

GAMBIER ISLANDS

AUSTRAL ISLANDS
PITCAIRN ISLAND

EASTER ISLAND

EAN

Pacific Ocean

STRANGERS
IN
PARADISE

STRANGERS IN PARADISE

MARTIN SUTTON

Angus&Robertson
An imprint of HarperCollins*Publishers*

DEDICATED TO:

My mother, Florence, and my late father, Arthur,
both of whom inspired my love of travel

Angus&Robertson
An imprint of HarperCollins*Publishers*, Australia

First published in Australia in 1995

Copyright © Martin Sutton 1995

This book is copyright.
Apart from any fair dealing for the purposes of
private study, research, criticism or review,
as permitted under the Copyright Act, no part
may be reproduced by any process without written permission.

Every effort has been made to contact the owners of copyright.
The publishers would welcome any further information regarding
holders of copyright not acknowledged.

HarperCollins*Publishers*
25 Ryde Road, Pymble, Sydney NSW 2073, Australia
31 View Road, Glenfield, Auckland 10, New Zealand
77–85 Fulham Palace Road, London W6 8JB, United Kingdom
Hazelton Lanes, 55 Avenue Road, Suite 2900, Toronto, Ontario M5R 3L2
and 1995 Markham Road, Scarborough, Ontario M1B 5M8, Canada
10 East 53rd Street, New York NY 10032, USA

National Library of Australia Cataloguing-in-Publication data:

Sutton, Martin, 1947–.
Strangers in paradise: adventurers and dreamers in the South Seas.

ISBN 0 207 18414 3.
1.Europeans – Oceania. 2.Missions – Oceania. 3.Missionaries – Oceania.
4.Oceania – History. 5.Oceania – Discovery and exploration.
I.Title.
996

Front cover background photograph of Tahiti courtesy of GIE Tahiti Tourism, Europe;
black and white photograph of Robert Louis Stevenson, his family and servants,
courtesy of the National Library of Australia, Canberra

Author photograph courtesy of W. J. M. Dawson

Half title page: The famous South Seas' head-dress *Hibiscus rosa-sinensis*, 1770, by Sydney Parkinson

Maps by Darian Causby

Printed in Hong Kong

9 8 7 6 5 4 3 2 1   99 98 97 96 95

Savages, ignorant savages,
have taught us thoroughly civilized beings a great,
great deal about the art of living and being happy.

PAUL GAUGUIN, 1893

ACKNOWLEDGEMENTS

I especially wish to thank Mark for his support and advice throughout, and my agent,
Caroline Davidson, for putting me on the right track.
Additionally, along the way, invaluable help has been given by my friends Geoff Gardner,
Jacqui Poulain and Anthony Allison.
Thanks also for the support and interest of all my friends at Ealing Central Library.

And thank you, Bengt.

◆ ◆ ◆

I am also indebted to the British Library and the Interlending Department of Ealing Libraries,
London, for access to most of the material referred to or quoted in this book.

CONTENTS

Traditional island dances, such as the hula, were notorious for their explicit eroticism

UTOPIA

IN THE PACIFIC

PARADISE, EDEN, LYONESSE, the Islands of the Blest, Atlantis, Elysium, Arcadia, Utopia, Shangri-La, Avalon … a few of the richly evocative names we have given to those legendary earthly places, or states, which we imagine as idyllic perfection. Here, all the perceived faults of our present society, physical and psychological, are cast out. Utopias are usually found in the form of a literary wish-fulfillment, or the theoretical groundplan for a future perfect. When visitors first set foot on the shores of Tahiti, however, they brought back the astonishing news that they had actually discovered a real heaven-on-earth which existed outside the pages of a book.

Utopias are found in all ages and cultures, almost as if the desire for heaven and earth to be united were part of the collective unconscious. It was once believed, for instance, that the Garden of Eden, from which Adam and Eve were expelled for bad behaviour, still existed somewhere on earth. Christopher Columbus was convinced he had discovered it at the mouth of the Orinoco in Venezuela, where four rivers met, as the Bible had described (Genesis 2:10). Indeed, the fact that utopia must exist 'elsewhere' led to a direct connection between voyages of discovery and the supposed location of earthly paradise.

One of the most important links between geographical discovery and a plan for paradise was that of the expeditions of Amerigo Vespucci to the New World and Sir Thomas More's *Utopia* (1516). More spoke to Raphael Hythloday, a member of Vespucci's crew, whose account of their adventures formed the basis of More's ideas. More even coined the term 'utopia' from the Greek 'ou' (not) and 'topos' (a place). His philosophical invention exerted a profound and subtle influence upon the culture of his day, placing him in the company of other eminent humanists of the Renaissance.

By the time the Americas were beginning to lose their hold upon the imagination of Europe, an ideal world was found again in the balmier regions of the South Pacific. Like More's Utopia, Tahiti was also an island and, in response to the romantic classical notions of the day, explorer Louis-Antoine de Bougainville called it Nouvelle Cythere, after the Greek island (Kythira) off whose coast Aphrodite, goddess of love, was born. In this case, however, the features of the imagined utopia had prior existence to the discovery of the island itself. They were to be found in the form of Jean-Jacques Rousseau's *Discourse on the Origin and Foundations of Inequality Among Men* (1755).

In this work, Rousseau paints a picture of an untainted, primitive world where man is 'eating his fill under an oak tree, quenching his thirst at the first stream, making his bed at the foot of the same tree which furnished his meal, with all his needs satisfied'. These early people were solitary beings with no responsibilities, other than to make love and raise the children until they could look after themselves. Having no knowledge of sin, they were 'neither good nor evil and had neither vices nor virtues'. Therefore, 'man is naturally good,' and there is an equality between individuals — that is, until the ownership of land, the serpent in Rousseau's Garden of Eden. Thus was born the ideal of the 'noble savage', living in rustic harmony with nature. Rousseau's passion for the wild, natural beauty of Corsica led him to idealize such landscapes, and he held that, 'Cities are the abyss of the human species.' This is not merely an aesthetic reaction, but a realistic reflection of the overcrowded, squalid nature of the cities of the period.

On a number of levels Rousseau had prepared explorers of his time for what they encountered. In the people of Oceania, Western idealists found a much closer approximation to the paradise of the philosopher–dreamers than had been previously discovered. Africans, Caribs, Aztecs, Incas and North American Indians were all not quite up to the standard set by European utopian thought of the time. Tahitians, however, were a beautiful, friendly, simple race, living in blissful contentment on a ravishingly beautiful island. They appeared to be living, breathing proof of the theories of Rousseau, as if they had conveniently sprung forth from the pages of his *Discourse*.

It was, and still is, quite startling to what extent parts of Polynesia, and Tahiti in particular, bear out this groundplan for paradise. On the islands, because there was plenty for everyone, and they knew no other life, no one went without and no one wanted more. As Rousseau says of his primitives, there was no place in the life of the Polynesians for such sins as envy, avarice and selfishness. Their religion, with its supreme god Te Atua, did not take it for granted that mankind was sinful. There was also no such thing as private property as we understand the term, since family ownership was spread very widely across huge, extended family systems. There was, thus, an amazing degree of equality.

Just as Rousseau's primitives slept beneath the tree which had fed them in the day, the islanders simply cast a net in the lagoon or reached up into a tree for a meal, later sleeping either beside their canoe or beneath a palm, if this was cooler than upon a mat indoors. They had one of the healthiest diets in the world, too, consisting of fruit and vegetables, fish and shellfish, and the occasional pig. The basic food, however, was the invaluable breadfruit, which the Europeans had not previously encountered. There was no doubt that all this was responsible for their flawless complexions, sturdy physiques and perfect teeth. They looked like gods beside the crews of the earlier ships, with their pasty Western complexions, bad teeth and ragged, unwashed appearance. The Tahitians washed several times a day in the many small streams that made their island verdant, dressed their hair with coconut oil, and both sexes loved to wear a flower behind the ear. The shabby, malodorous crews must have seemed offensive to these people.

Despite those 'sinful' faults which the Church in particular blamed them for, Polynesians were a compassionate, sympathetic race. Although they stole from all the visiting ships, they also gave in abundance — food, ethnological objects and their sexual favours. They always freely expressed their emotions, men as much as women. They would burst into tears when members of a crew were flogged, attempting to stop the process, and were not able to grasp how such harshness could be justified. They were also overcome with remorse when the ships left, wailing and crying on the beaches long after the vessels were out of sight.

Europeans, and the Church in particular, looked upon the islanders as lazy. Even a visiting writer as liberal-minded as Herman Melville accused them of 'an indolence, bodily and mentally'. It is true that they could not appreciate the Western ethic of work as a virtue in itself. As with so many of their qualities, however, it is misleading to judge them by the standards of another culture. They did everything which was useful for their lives — gardening, the making of nets and fishing lines from coconut fibre, the simple making of clothes from the beaten bark of trees, and the preparation of food. But Nature was kind in the South Seas, and toil as such was unnecessary. What work there was to be done, was also done for oneself, and — as early colonists and the missionaries were frustrated to discover — the islanders could not easily be made to see the sense of labour for others.

The resultant existence was one of delicious, sensual languor. It was necessary to sleep through the hottest part of the day, and frequent, lazy swims cooled them off pleasurably. When it was cooler, they enjoyed activities such as archery, climbing trees, racing, body-surfing, dancing and making love. Some visiting writers understood all this perfectly. French sailor and novelist Pierre Loti admired the Tahitian lifestyle of 'utter idleness and perpetual dreaming', and an amused American poet, Charles Warren Stoddard, saw it as 'a picture of still-life with the suggestion of possible motion'. Only the sturdiest advocates of the work ethic could fail to appreciate that in much of Oceania 'work' and 'pleasure' had become delightfully, idyllically confused. Surely this was the Garden of Eden, where God had all but removed the burden of toil from the shoulders of mankind?

Rousseau's antipathy to towns and cities was also taken up as a Tahitian theme. As visiting American journalist Frederick O'Brien noted as late as 1915: 'The Tahitian never lived in hamlets, as the Marquesan and the Samoan, but each family dwelt in its wood of coco-nuts and breadfruit, or a few families clustered their inhabitants for intimacy and mutual aid.' The coming of the missionary, the storekeeper and foreign governments broke up this individualistic social pattern. The islanders could be controlled, made to think like sheep in a pen, it was discovered, only by bringing them together into social centres.

Far and away the paramount obsession the West had with the South Seas was sex. On this subject, at least, the utopian philosophers had not correctly pre-empted Oceanic practice. Rousseau believed that primitives had the sexual urge in its pure, unromantic, most unproblematic form. 'The moral aspect of love is an artificial sentiment, born of social custom,' he wrote. Thomas More's state of utopia depicts sex in equally pragmatic terms, for in his paradise men and women strip off for each other before taking the plunge into married life. Polynesians, however, did fall in love. Even so, the theme of an uncomplicated, casual enjoyment of the act itself does relate to the experience of early visitors to the islands.

Observed by a foreign culture that seldom attempted to understand the Polynesian way of life, the islanders' unselfconscious enjoyment of erotic pleasure was frankly shocking. To relish intercourse as one would delight in a meal seemed almost animal. However, there could be no sin where no guilt existed, no sense of the prurient and no shyness. For the islanders, sex was simply a wonderful gift to be shared.

As soon as they were old enough to understand, they were taught all about this wonderful faculty they had been granted, and when they were old enough to enjoy it, they were encouraged to practise. They soon developed sexual skills and a lack of inhibition which may have startled many a Westerner. And they would share their sexual favours as they would their food and homes. When someone married, they married into the whole, vast, extended family in a very real sense. Rather confounding Rousseau, there was indeed romance but, as a result of this open system, little jealousy or possessiveness. Where taboos did exist, they merely banned incest and discouraged sex across the classes — between a chief's family and his people. Early visitors to the islands were astonished at the toleration of gay sexuality — the traditional acceptance of the male homosexual, or 'mahu', continuing through to our times.

The Tahitian's lack of inhibitions was one thing that startled the crews of the early ships. A customary method of greeting, for both males and females, was to remove the top half of one's clothes, rather as we would take off our gloves and hat. This made the sailors on board Bougainville's ship feel very welcome indeed. No sooner had they dropped anchor at Tahiti than a young woman slipped aboard:

> *The young girl casually allowed her pagne [loin-cloth] to fall to the ground and appeared to all eyes as Venus did to the Phrygian shepherd. She had the Goddess's celestial form. Sailors and soldiers hurried to get to the hatchway, and never was capstan heaved with such speed.*

By the same token, the islanders frequently encouraged the sailors to undress before them, out of sheer inquisitiveness to see if everything was in the right place. As Bougainville reported: 'The boldest among them came to touch us; they even pushed aside our clothes with their hands, in order to see whether we were made exactly like them.' It must, indeed, have seemed puzzling to the islanders who wore so little, why these visitors covered themselves from head to foot in sweaty cocked hats, sometimes wigs, ruffled shirts, breeches, stockings and buckled shoes. What had they to hide?

There was also no bashfulness when it came to where, and in front of whom, one actually made love. Under a palm tree, on the beach, or on a mat in a hut suited equally. Early visitors were frequently diffident, though, about performing with a friendly, interested group looking on. The audience, however, were not prurient, merely eager to encourage the ecstasy and to see if they could learn anything novel from their guests.

Related to the Westerners' obsession with Polynesian promiscuity was their reverence for the women of the islands. True to national stereotype, French commander Bougainville was one of the earliest and most ardent admirers of Polynesian womanhood, the 'vahine'. It was the general habit of these ladies to swim out to approaching ships without a stitch on, and clamber aboard, shielded immodestly with only the strands of their long wet hair. American seaman and future novelist Herman Melville was horrified at this bold behaviour, but Bougainville merely reflected approvingly that they were 'the equal of the majority of European women'. The crews in general were overcome by the general standard of island female beauty, and some members were only torn away from their native sweethearts by force. In this respect, the case of the *Bounty* is infamous, where virtually an entire crew mutineered rather than bear separation from their Tahitian lovers.

The charm of the island women became legendary back home, even to those who could not read, through the sensational tales spread about by the returning sailors. Even the rather conservative artist on board Cook's final voyage, John Webber, painted a fabulous, erotic portrait of a lovely Polynesian girl, Poedua, with her pareu (sarong) pulled down to expose her breasts in friendly native greeting. Images such as this excited crowds at the major galleries and were reproduced endlessly.

Of course, there were dissenting voices in the midst of the clamour — though few listened. One of the earliest was William Wales, strait-laced astronomer on Cook's second voyage. He considered the beauty of the Tahitian women vastly overrated, and found the native dance, the hula, 'too ludicrous to be pleasing'. Later, Charles Darwin adjusted the usual emphasis by admitting to being 'much disappointed in the personal appearance of the women: they are far inferior in every respect to the men'. Gauguin, who painted many Tahitian women, and even married one, thought them in general 'androgynous'. It was an opinion over which English poet Rupert Brooke later took the painter to task. Was all this divergence just churlish carping, or did the gentlemen really have a point? The evidence would certainly seem overwhelming against them.

None the less, most male visitors to the islands seem to have been transfixed by Polynesian women — and one of them, Charles Warren Stoddard, by several of the men. In literary circles, Stoddard, Herman Melville, Pierre Loti and Rupert Brooke were moved to immortalise their island lovers. Melville, at first stupefied by the women's forwardness, soon succumbed to their allure. Of his beloved Marquesan Fayaway, he wrote: 'The face of this girl was a rounded oval, and each feature as perfectly formed as the heart or imagination of man could desire.' (*Typee*). Loti was no less struck by the diminutive Tahitian Rarahu, whose 'eyes were of a tawny black, full of exotic languor and coaxing softness'. (*The Marriage of Loti*). Mamua, Brooke's slice of Tahitian paradise, was 'a girl with wonderful eyes, the walk of a goddess, and the heart of an angel'. (*Letters*). As for Stoddard, who visited Tahiti and Hawaii several times between 1864 and 1873, the islands were as kind to this gay writer as to anyone else. His Hawaiian companion, Kana-ana, proved to be someone not easily forgotten: 'His sleek figure, supple and graceful in repose, was the embodiment of free, untrammelled youth.' (*South-Sea Idyls*).

The impression made by these real-life islanders upon the European literary scene was electrifying. The exotic and seductive portraits of Fayaway and Rarahu became exemplars, for instance, for Robert Louis Stevenson's Uma ('The Beach of Falesa'), Somerset Maugham's Ethel ('The Pool'), Nordhoff and Hall's Tehani (*Mutiny on the Bounty*), Zane Grey's Faaone (*The Reef Girl*) and James A. Michener's Liat (*Tales of the South Pacific*). Furthermore, following Loti and Melville, not to mention the crews of the early explorers, the South Seas mistress or wife became the vogue. Although generally overlooked at the time, the *Bounty* writing team of Nordhoff and Hall, and American novelist Robert Dean Frisbie, all quietly enjoyed long and happy marriages to their Polynesian brides earlier this century, completely fulfilling their romantic dreams of the South Seas. Less happily, but more famously, both Gauguin and Marlon Brando found brief attachments to Tahitian women — the former with Tehamana, the artist's frequent model, and the latter with Tarita Teriipia, the actor's co-star in *Mutiny on the Bounty* (1962).

American author Robert Dean Frisbie and his children on the Cook island of Puka-Puka in the 1920s

An intriguing addition to this list of island amours is the only publicized example of a smitten

Western female. Fifty-four-year-old Los Angeles-born Joana McIntyre Varawa fell for a Fijian fisherman less than half her age when she went looking for South Sea adventure in the 1980s. Her feistiness, and enchantment with island life, is chronicled in her delightful autobiography *Changes in Latitude: An Uncommon Anthropology* (1990).

By the time Cook's third circumnavigation was completed, Europe had the facts and the time to reflect upon those aspects of island life that did not really vie with all the utopian visions. The Tahitians, it seemed, indulged in theft, warfare, human sacrifice and infanticide. The first two, while

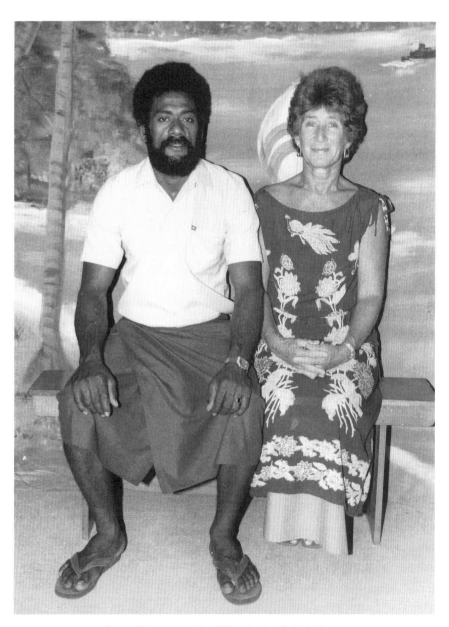

Joana McIntyre and her Fijian husband, Male Varawa

not indeed reflecting paradise, were perhaps forgiveably prosaic, because so very familiar to the societies of the visitors themselves. Even so, all these 'sins' were generally misunderstood, being judged from the perspective of Western standards.

To begin with, inter-island warfare was very far from the prolonged, epic spectacle of mass slaughter which was the style in many more 'civilized' parts of the world. In the main, Tahitians fought each other in considerably scaled-down squabbles and differences of opinion. Indeed, the Polynesian character was in general quite gentle and sensitive. On Cook's second voyage, for example, he found it very difficult to be impressed by the enormously tall and dignified figure of Tu, whom the crew took to be overall regent of the island. Tu, 6 foot 3 (190.5 centimetres) and still under twenty, recoiled from swords and guns, displaying a timidity which the visitors thought unbecoming to his sex.

Theft, which was even more misunderstood, was found by early explorers to be widespread throughout the Pacific islands. The Spaniards had actually christened the Marianas the Ladrones — Islands of Thieves — after their experiences there. Bougainville observed, with admiration, that the skill of the Tahitians was worthy of the finest Parisian pickpockets. It was noted, though, that the islanders did not steal from each other. The main reason for this was that they lacked the Westerner's notion of private property. They very freely loaned or gave anything to one another. Thus, when they took objects from the visitors, it was not with the intention of making these things exclusively their own. Besides, the strangers to their island freely helped themselves to food, water and trees for wood, which was a much more final form of possession. The visitors also had in mind the ultimate form of theft — to own the islands themselves and all their inhabitants, body and soul.

The issues of human sacrifice and infanticide were much thornier subjects. Cook, who himself had attended a sacrifice, did not attempt to judge what he saw as one of the dark mysteries of Polynesian religion. It was not, anyway, a common requirement of their gods, taking place only to try to ensure triumph in battle. And infanticide occurred, for example, when a baby was born to a member of a chief's family and a commoner. Such a birth was taboo.

Although several of the more empathetic visitors to the South Seas attempted to defend these practices when they returned home, in general there was no attempt to see such actions from any point of view other than the Western. Such an attitude especially profited the Church, who viewed the veneration of Polynesia as a direct threat to the moral precepts of Christianity. Others, of a conservative nature and in positions of power, saw all this talk of utopian equality as a threat to their own society's stability, and were therefore thankful that shortcomings could be found in this vision of Edenic perfection.

There also seemed, in all this fault-finding, almost a touch of jealousy. Why should these islanders be having such fun, when our lives are so grey and forbidding? In this light, the cruel imposition of Western values upon the islanders resembles a form of retribution.

From Bougainville to Brando, all this South Sea dreaming was kindled, as we have seen, by the fortuitous overlapping of Rousseau's utopian ideas with the discovery of the islands. To fully

A sketch of Papeete, Tahiti, made by British artist Conway Sharples in 1848. Standing in its own garden
is the royal palace, and Moorea can be seen on the horizon

appreciate the tremendous impact of the South Seas idyll upon eighteenth-century Europe, one must take into account the everyday life of the period. Due to improvements in the areas of medicine, agriculture and science, the population of Europe had doubled during the century from 90 to 180 million, which put a strain on both urban and rural communities. Unemployment in country areas led to workers flooding into the towns and cities. By the end of the century, over one million people dwelt in London, with 70,000 in Paris. A working-class family usually lived in one room, and unmarried women frequently turned to prostitution.

Besides these physical conditions, there was an atmosphere of religious intolerance and governmental corruption. Freethinkers stood the risk of imprisonment or execution for their beliefs, particularly from a dogmatic Church. For those who could afford the passage, the British colonies in North America formed an attractive escape route from grinding poverty, overcrowding, narrow-mindedness and the grim working conditions of the steadily expanding industrial revolution.

Into such a world came stories of a place gloriously dissimilar, though terribly far away. From the dockyards, even into the slums, spread golden visions of a heaven on earth. It must have galled a little, but it was also strangely reassuring. Somewhere, at least, there was a place where the sun shone all year, food was everywhere for the taking, people did not labour for others, streams ran through sylvan groves into emerald lagoons, everyone was more or less equal and free, there was no shame, and the possibilities for sexual adventure were almost boundless. This was perhaps the most potent of utopias, arising in just the right place at just the right time. Access to this knowledge was certainly not just restricted to the educated middle and upper classes.

The working classes in England dreamed of all this magic in the midst of their dissatisfaction. In France, however, it made the disadvantaged angry, allowed educated liberals to see that Rousseau seemed to have a point, and was probably one of the influences in leading people to take to the streets in an attempt to bring about a new order. Not that the discovery of Tahiti brought about the French Revolution, but it certainly proved an unexpectedly subversive force in that direction.

Even utopias obey the laws of fashion, however. The headlines of today are the middle section of tomorrow. After 1800, when the wilderness of the American West was opened up, utopia was seen for a time to reside in the huge grassy plains and beautiful leafy valleys of this untouched land. But as more remote and virgin territories were opened up across the face of the planet, so the search for true paradise became more desperate. As astronomy and science grew in stature, utopians were even encouraged to seek the perfect world in outer space itself. Today, much science fiction posits an extraterrestrial Shangri-La for precisely this reason. For a great many dreamers, though, the scatter of islands across the vast waters of the Pacific is still space-travel enough. The legend of the South Seas is a dream that has not been extinguished.

Beside the pale, scrawny and dishevelled appearance of the European crews, the tall, natural,
healthy look of the islanders enhanced their image as gods of a new-found utopia

From Cook's final voyage, John Webber's portrait of the fifteen-year-old Polynesian dancing girl,
Poedooa, Daughter of Orea, Chief of Ulietea

Early visitors to the islands greatly admired the simple beauty of the cool

native houses shaded by palm trees

An anonymous coloured pencil drawing, Tahitians Presenting Fruit to Bougainville

CHAPTER ONE

SEARCHING

FOR EDEN

ON 28TH NOVEMBER 1520, the Portuguese navigator Ferdinand Magellan, under contract to Spain, entered the great rolling ocean which he named the Pacific. It represented a major breakthrough in the control of the Spice Routes from the Molucca islands of Indonesia. From this moment until the end of the sixteenth century, Spanish navigators criss-crossed the region, discovering many of the major islands and groups, such as New Guinea, the Marshalls, the Marianas, the New Hebrides, the Solomons, the Marquesas, Santa Cruz and the Tuamotus. They even set foot on Hawaii 200 years before Cook.

Chiefly, they were searching for the mythical Terra Australis Incognita, a huge southern continent intriguingly hinted at in Inca legend and in the voyages of King Solomon's ships recorded in the Bible. It was believed to be a blissful paradise akin to the Garden of Eden. In 1605, explorer and religious fanatic Pedro Ferdinand de Quiros thought he had found it and named the likely island Australia del Espiritu Santo (today, plain Espiritu Santo, in Vanuatu). The continent that actually best fitted the bill in terms of size and geography, however, was discovered a year later when Dutchman Willem Jansz sailed past the west coast of Australia's Queensland.

The difficulty was that inexact methods of measurement (no instrument would exist to calculate longitude correctly until 1775) resulted in these early discoveries remaining virtually untraceable. It was as if the islands themselves floated about, subject to the same vagaries of weather as the ships themselves.

By 1750, conditions had changed. For a start, ships were generally much larger than the Spanish caravels and carracks of the earlier explorers, being between 300 and 600 tons. They carried enough sail to cope with all types of weather, and could contain supplies for several years in their yawning holds. To help ward off scurvy, the scourge of long sea voyages, the food supplies on Cook's first voyage included such vitamin-rich items as sauerkraut, wild greens and malt. There was also a more systematic, less haphazard purpose in circumnavigation, with more all-round preparation. However, by now the 'useful' sea routes had been explored, and these later voyages were undertaken in a more relaxed spirit of scientific enquiry. European cultural movements of the age also meant that these more leisurely, inquisitive travellers were embarking upon voyages of enchantment, rather than upon religious odysseys or trade missions.

Two of the first crews on the scene in this later period were British. The first of these was the *Dolphin*, which was under the command of John Byron, grandfather of the future poet. The ship entered the Pacific in April 1765, but shot through the region with apparent disinterest, touching only a few of the northernmost islands, and reached Java in the November. Byron had not the nose for sniffing out these isolated specks of land, and did not even take the bother to zigzag across the map in the prescribed manner of the maritime explorer. None the less, his grandson used the account of the voyage in scenes for his poem *Don Juan*.

Now copper-sheathed against shipworm, the *Dolphin* enjoyed a second airing in the Pacific under the command of the far more inquisitive, though often unwell, Samuel Wallis. Opening up an area of the Pacific not previously discovered, on the morning of the 18th June 1766, the ship was at anchor in the slowly dispersing mists of Tahiti's Matavai Bay. It was seen to be surrounded by a hundred canoes, but the unfriendly reception was terminated abruptly by the appearance on deck of one of the ship's goats — which seemed a fearsome creature to the islanders, who had never come across one before. Friendly relations were established and Wallis, unimaginatively, dubbed his find King George the Third Island. Queen Oberea welcomed him to her palace, where her handmaidens treated the astonished captain to a massage. As for the crew, they were the first to bargain for sexual favours with nails, highly prized by the Tahitians. When the ship sailed, after a month, the Queen and the women wept on the shore.

A year later, on 6th April 1768, Louis Antoine de Bougainville entered Hitiaa Bay, on the east side of Tahiti. Dignified, scholarly and aristocratic, this French navigator was already famous in England. At twenty-seven he had written the influential *Treatise on Integral Calculus*, and had proved himself a gifted commanding officer by negotiating the surrender of Quebec, finding a colony for the displaced Nova Scotians and organising an investigative voyage to the Falklands. The crowning glory of his career, however, was his voyage to the Pacific, particularly the scant ten days he spent on Tahiti.

Symptomatic of the tone of his entire Tahitian sojourn, his ship, the 550-ton frigate *La Boudeuse*, was greeted in friendly fashion by a hundred native pirogues filled with green boughs, fruit and fowl. Presumably the islanders recalled the pleasant stay of Captain Wallis. There were, however, other gifts in the canoes, as Bougainville reported:

Women whose beauty was the equal of the majority of European women. Most of these nymphs were nude ... The men urged us to choose a woman and follow her ashore ... I ask you: given such a spectacle, how could one keep at work four hundred Frenchmen — young sailors who had not seen a woman in six months?

And thus, on this day was born the legend of Tahiti, Isle of Love.

Bougainville had indeed, to all intents and purposes, found an authentically arcadian bower. From the moment the ship first entered the shelter of the bay, he had been overawed by the peaceful beauty of the island's cascading waterfalls, lush green peaks and the charming thatched houses built in the shade of the palm and fruit trees. He quickly grew to love the island and its people, tolerated their pilfering and calmly defused any confrontations with his men. He was once serenaded with nose-flute and folk songs while sitting beneath the shade of a palm tree. He was also most charmingly propositioned: 'The Chief offered me one of his women, young and fairly pretty, and the entire assembly sang the marriage hymn. What a country! What a people!'

It would be true to say that Bougainville saw the island and its people at their very best. Much is made by commentators of his naïve romanticism, but he was a scholar first and foremost, noting down details of custom and government, as well as compiling a rough dictionary, which he later published. We can assume, therefore, that what

Tarita's scanty sarong and lei for the 1962 film Mutiny on the Bounty *would be the style in which early crews were greeted by Polynesian women*

Louis-Antoine, Comte de Bougainville (1729–1811), the brilliant young French captain who first invested Tahiti with its romantic image

he reported was what he saw, despite some period propensity for flowery description. Bougainville could hardly be blamed for the fact that during his ten-day stay there was no war, infanticide, cannibalism or human sacrifice — some of which Cook later experienced during his longer visits. The Frenchman merely saw instead the islanders getting on with their lives on a day-to-day basis. What he was saying, beneath all the fashionable European clichés of the age, was that workaday life on the islands was far, far more enchanting than the everyday grind back home.

He was not blinded to the faults of the islanders, such as theft, but likened these, rather patronizingly perhaps, to the imperfections of children. But beside these peccadilloes, the virtues of the islanders seemed glowing:

Though the island is divided into many little districts, each of which has its own master, yet there does not seem to be any civil war, or any private hatred on the isle … Their houses are always open. Everyone gathers fruit from the first tree he meets with … It should seem as if, in regard to things absolutely necessary for the maintenance of life, there was no personal property amongst them, and that they all had equal right to these articles.

An incident took place during his time on Tahiti which quite sets the voyage apart from the experiences of other circumnavigators. Entirely in keeping with the extravagant romance of the setting, the natives discovered something intriguing about a member of the crew. The personal valet of Philibert Commerson, the ship's doctor and naturalist, no sooner set foot on shore than 'all the savages began to pull at him and again and again cry "Ayenene! Ayenene!"[girl]'. What no member of the crew had yet discovered was that Commerson's valet was in fact a young woman named Jeanne Baret, quite possibly the first female

Captain Bougainville moored on the windward side of Tahiti and lost six anchors in ten days due to the fierce currents. This one was only recently salvaged, by a man from the village of Hitiaa, in whose bay the captain anchored

aboard a circumnavigating vessel. To try to protect the doctor, she pretended that he, too, was unaware of her ruse. Needless to say, few underestimated his insight in such matters, and it transpired that the couple had been partners for two years.

As the time for departure neared, Bougainville left parting gifts of geese and turkeys, and a garden planted with French vegetables. Claiming the island for France, he named it Nouvelle Cythere (New Cythera), clearly showing far more imagination than Wallis. As the ship headed for the passage in the reef, the Tahitians gave chase in their pirogues, beside themselves with anguish. Shedding tears, they offered gifts in the shape of supplies, and insisted that the expedition return with a real-life memento, Ahu-Toru, the son of an island chief. On the voyage back, however, this middle-aged Tahitian rather took the bloom off the paradise they had just witnessed by informing them that Tahiti was like everywhere else in sometimes settling conflicts through war.

Back in Paris, Bougainville was fêted, not least for the coup of having secured a flesh-and-blood trophy. Ahu-Toru found himself received at court, and was quickly adopted by the Duchesse de Choiseul, who showed him off in every salon in the city. It is said that in the eleven months he spent there, he became so familiar with Paris that he would wander the city by himself and never get lost. But, rather like an old toy, Ahu-Toru was soon cast aside by a city which had grown tired of the novelty. He never learned to speak French, and his unprepossessing appearance failed to vie with the capital's preconceptions of a citizen from New Cythera.

Bougainville published *The Voyage Around the World* in 1771, which proved the most fashionable book of its time in every salon. The following year, Diderot wrote a supplement to the book, refuting its idealism, but this had a limited circulation. In order to win a wider readership, Bougainville had deliberately left out any scientific detail — despite all the hydrographic charts, naturalist notebooks and records of longitude which resulted from the voyage. The negative implications of this were compounded by the fact that, after Commerson's death in 1773, his copious notes on flora and fauna somehow remained unpublished, just as his collection of specimens was dispersed.

Ultimately, the scientific benefits of Bougainville's voyage were quite wasted. However, each new venture built upon the experiences and hard-won breakthroughs of those which went before. The next circumnavigation would be better prepared and more self-conscious of its mission. Ironically, for all his achievements and dignified humanity, Bougainville's chief claim to fame lies in lending his name to bougainvillea, the sumptuous purple blooms which the expedition discovered cascading across houses in Uruguay's capital, Montevideo.

The most important of all South Sea explorers was Captain Cook (1728–79), who undertook three trailblazing voyages to the region. He was a self-taught sailor, from a Yorkshire agricultural family, who had worked his way up through the ranks of hydrographer and deep-sea pilot. He was infamous for being disconcertingly curt of manner and tough and inflexible when it came to rules, but was held in great esteem for the concern he always showed for his crews. As for his ship, for the first voyage (1768–71) the *Endeavour* was a refitted coastal bark of 366 tons. Designed originally for the transport of coal, it was, like its captain, to enjoy an altogether more adventurous and glamorous career than its origins would suggest.

This first voyage was undertaken ostensibly to measure the transit of Venus to determine the earth's distance from the sun as a navigational aid. Additionally, Cook and the crew were asked to keep a look out for Terra Australis Incognita. Wallis himself had suggested 'King George Island' as the best place to observe this astronomical event, and the ship anchored in Matavai Bay on 11th April 1769. Their reception was friendly and Joseph Banks, the leader of the naturalist team, found the scene blissfully arcadian. However, various incidents of pickpocketing led to the shooting of one islander, as Cook proved much less able to defuse confrontations than Bougainville. (This may, in part, account for the fatal encounter on a beach in Hawaii which climaxed his third voyage.)

Fortunately, Banks was on hand to help with the vital matter of a stolen octant (an astronomical instrument for measuring angles) which an islander had decided would make a fine souvenir. Banks's relationship with the Tahitians, particularly the young women, was very cordial, to say the least. Cook was by nature more formal and distant, and suffered jibes from the women for his celibacy. Although Cook did not himself indulge, he did not discourage his men from enjoying the carnal pleasures of the island. He even went as far as to allow the women on board at night throughout the *Endeavour*'s three-month stay.

The 'transit' was observed on 3rd June, as predicted, though departure was delayed by repairs. Two smitten men attempted to hide out on the island with their sweethearts, but they were sought out in time. When they eventually sailed on 13th July, there were more tears from the islanders, and quite a measure of reluctance from the love-struck men. Some forty islanders were also struck by venereal disease. Cook blamed Bougainville's crew for delivering this curse upon them and they, in turn, blamed Wallis.

The reception back home two years later was triumphant for everyone except Cook. The Royal Society was delighted with Banks, who had an audience with the King and an open invitation to all London society dinners. Dr Samuel Johnson even wrote a piece about the goat which had supplied the ship with milk. Cook, however, received only scant acknowledgement. Even the account of the voyage was written up from Cook's journals by fashionable journalist Dr John Hawkesworth. It was considered that Cook himself was too much the rude seaman to rise to such a task. The result of this misconception was a very free, romanticized version of the journals. *Hawkesworth's Voyages*, as the work came to be known, was actually more influenced in overall style by Banks's more fabulous descriptions than by Cook's fairly sober account.

Cook now had to suffer unwarranted broadsides from the critics. For one thing, Hawkesworth's glowing report of this lazy, sensual paradise was seen as an attack on the British concept of 'progress'. However, Hawkesworth's purple prose and his image of the permissive but 'noble savage' had tremendous appeal when the book was published in 1773. It was reprinted twice that year, and the following year translated into French, German and Italian. The popularity of such a bastardized version of the facts made it worse for the captain who, after just fourteen months back home, gratefully accepted an offer to command a second voyage (1772–75).

This time, the ship was the 462-ton bark *Resolution*, and the reason for the voyage was to search out that stubborn southern continent once again. On board were such novelties as carrot marmalade and concentrated beer to try to help combat scurvy, that most tenacious of enemies. As the ship entered the bay at Tahiti on 16th August 1773, naturalist Johann Rheinhold Forster noticed with delight the perfume of the island flowers which came to greet them on the breeze.

Since their last visit, antipathy had broken out between the main part of the island and its wilder, southernmost peninsula. Moreover, in the interim, a Spanish vessel had visited the island and infected the inhabitants with an unknown, fatal sickness. In a spirit of true sympathy and liberal-mindedness, Cook wrote:

> *We debauch their morals already too prone to vice and we introduce among them wants and perhaps diseases which they never before knew and which serve only to disturb that happy tranquillity they and their Fore-fathers had enjoyed. If anyone denies the truth of this assertion let him tell me what the Natives of the whole extent of America have gained by the commerce they had had with Europeans.*

After only a couple of weeks, the *Resolution* sailed on to visit Tonga, New Zealand, the Antarctic, Easter Island and the Marquesas, returning to Tahiti by late April 1774. This time, Forster undertook pioneering anthropological work on differences between the racial types, noting the beauty and carefree nature of the Polynesians and the artistic skills of the warlike Maoris. But such toil was not the norm for a stay which involved more festivities than ever. The women left the ship each morning proudly and shamelessly wearing the sailors' shirts. The Feast of Saint George on 23rd April was simply an excuse for more licence. A few days later, King Otoo organised a naval spectacle for Cook with 160 double canoes manned by Tahitians in war costume, with 170 smaller pirogues. All in all, there were some 7,000 men upon the waters of Matavai Bay.

Despite the generally riotous quality of this sojourn, as the date came near for departure (14th May), this time only one man attempted to jump ship. He was recovered but, oddly, Cook admitted that had the miscreant asked, he would have given his assent for the sailor to stay on. It seems that the islands were working their magic on even this stickler for regulations. Rather than losing a man, however, the voyagers actually returned with one extra. Picked up on Huahine, in the Society Islands, Omai was another living trophy like Bougainville's islander. Unlike Ahu-Toru, though, Omai had charm and an inquisitive intelligence which endeared him to most of those he met, and made him half-sorry to return to the islands. (He is considered in greater detail later on, with reference to Sir Joseph Banks.)

The second expedition had returned with wondrous treasures: a shrunken head, three Tahitian dogs, and all manner of what were referred to as 'artificial curiosities', as well as the more prosaic maps and charts, and cases of natural history specimens. This time Cook was befittingly honoured, and offered a post as captain at the Greenwich Hospital for disabled sailors. As for the published account of the voyage, after the last debacle, the public were this time allowed to read the report in the captain's own words: 'It is my own narrative, and it was written during the voyage.' The two volumes were eventually published in May 1777 with enormous success. Now, though, the erotic subjects that had formed the 'fruitier' passages in Hawkesworth, were not covered, for the sake of 'the nicest reader'.

Hardly had his feet touched terra firma, however, than he was asked to rediscover his sea-legs and dispatched to discover the Northwest Passage, a North American link between the Atlantic and the Pacific. The *Resolution* was made ready once more, and a wistful Omai given passage back home.

Cook's ill-fated final voyage (1776–80) set off to a promising start with the discovery of the exquisite archipelago, consisting mainly of atolls, that still bears his name. At Mangaia, the southernmost of the Cook Islands, they were met in friendly, if bizarre, fashion. The islanders repeatedly bade the crew strip off, examining their bodies in disgust and horror. To the brown-skinned inhabitants, flesh this white indicated the ghosts of dead ancestors.

At Anamooka (Nomuka), in the Friendly Isles (the Kingdom of Tonga), a feast, with mountains of fruit and roasted pigs, was held in their honour. As they ate, they watched boxing matches in which fearless young women took part. When challenged, members of the crew were quite unable to better these fierce Tongan pugilists. It is said that Cook's crew would have been on the menu themselves but for their conviviality. The captain even presented the King with a male Galapagos tortoise, a gift considered so sacred that the creature wandered about the royal gardens right up to 1966, when it died at the splendid age of 190. Before leaving, on Tongatapu, Cook noted the use of the new word 'taboo', used in connection with those who must not feed themselves for a period after dressing a corpse.

Zoffany's Death of Cook *was a dramatic recreation of the captain's final agonized moments on a Hawaiian beach*

By August 1777, Cook was anchored again in Matavai Bay. But this sojourn on Tahiti was far from the idyll it had previously been. The main island was at war with its smaller neighbour Eimeo (Moorea). Although invited to partake, Cook flatly refused to intervene. As a preliminary to the fighting, to placate the gods, a human sacrifice was held to which Cook was invited. The victim of such a ceremony was always killed first, attacked unawares with a fierce blow from behind. The unlucky person was either a known criminal or vagrant. Cook watched the ceremony with restrained horror, while being sketched by John Webber, the expedition's artist. At the event's grisly conclusion, the chief was offered the victim's eye, which he pretended to eat. This incident marked the beginning of a new stage in the perception of the islands, in which their air of romance was realistically modified.

Between September and December, they toured around the Society Islands, returning Omai to Huahine, where they built him a house and garden. They spent Christmas on the largest island of the Line archipelago, which they named after the festival itself and, by 20th January 1778, reached Kauai, in the Hawaiian islands. After also discovering Oahu, Niihau, Lanai and Kahoolawe, Cook named the group after the Earl of Sandwich. He was startled to discover that the inhabitants were Polynesian, a race which might not be the most numerous on the planet, but were certainly one of the farthest spread. For their part, the islanders had clearly never seen a vessel like the *Resolution*, and undoubtedly regarded their visitors as supernatural beings.

Between February and August, Cook searched without success for the Northwest Passage. Returning to the Sandwich (Hawaiian) Islands, they found Maui and the Big Island, and anchored at the charming Kealakekua Bay on the latter. Here they were overwhelmed with inquisitive natives clambering aboard, and were forced to fire guns to keep order. At this point in the journals of Cook, the great captain ceases his account, being replaced by the voice of Second Lt. James King. It was King's sad duty to conclude the tragic story.

The bay's name translates as 'the path of the gods', and the islanders concluded that Cook, being in charge of this strange vessel of supernatural beings, must be the great Orono, god of peace and prosperity. However, as storms locked the ship into the bay, the friction between crew and islanders worsened. An incident over a stolen canoe led to a skirmish in which Cook was stabbed in the back. Even this display of ungodlike mortality did not, however, diminish Cook's supernatural significance for those who killed him. Only some of Cook's bones were eventually returned to the ship, the remainder of them forming the focus of religious worship up until 1820, when the first missionaries arrived.

If Cook had been mistaken for a god by the islanders, back home he was taken to be a martyr. The account of the last voyage, freely edited by Canon Douglas in 1784, sold out in just three days, and a second edition was immediately published. Artists sometimes depicted the captain, fallen, with one hand raised to his murderers, in a saintly gesture almost of forgiveness. The London stage spectacle *Omai*, and the Paris equivalent *La mort du Capitaine Cook*, were quite the theatrical vogue, concluding with the man raised up to heaven by Genius and Fame. Certainly, between them, Tahiti and Hawaii had now fallen foul of the peaceful arcadian image once ascribed to them.

The visionary French were amongst Cook's most fervent fans. The most enthusiastic was Louis XVI. Every Frenchman had gloried in the style and verve of Bougainville's South Sea enterprise, but France still needed a well-planned voyage to equal the full splendour of Cook's achievements.

The first Frenchman chosen to attempt such a task, while Cook was still on his first voyage, was French India Company employee Jean Francois Marie de Surville. He sailed from India aboard the *Saint-Jean-Baptiste* in late 1769, finding only one of the Solomon Islands, and losing many men to scurvy and desertion. In 1771, Marion du Fresne left France on the *Mascarin* to return Ahu-Toru home. He discovered the Marion and Crozet Islands, south-east of Cape Town, but was murdered in New Zealand and some of the crew died from scurvy. This terrible misfortune was to dog French exploration in a far more spectacular fashion with the extraordinarily disastrous voyage of La Pérouse.

Jean-Francois de Galaup, Comte de la Pérouse, sailed from Brest in August 1785 on the 500-ton frigate *La Boussole*, on a voyage that was intended to be extensively scientific. In the hold were thousands of hatchets and combs as gifts for the islanders. They reached Easter Island in April 1786, though the reception here was not as friendly as the one that Cook had enjoyed. Even the native women were at first hidden, then later introduced, with various lewd gestures, to indicate that their favours were for sale. After only a few hours, the ship headed north, reaching the Hawaiian island of Maui by the end of May. The first taste of trouble occurred two months later, when two longboats and their men were lost in the strong currents of an Alaskan bay.

By September they headed back across the Pacific, touching the Marianas, and spending a year reconnoitring the coasts of China and Russia. In December 1787, they came across the Navigator Islands (Samoa), which at first enchanted them as greatly as Tahiti had touched Bougainville. Anchored at Tutuila, they believed the Samoans 'the happiest people in the world', and the hilly green island to be heaven on earth. Upon closer inspection, however, the preponderance of battle scars on the bodies of the natives, and their delight in theft, made the visitors eager to leave. They were not fast enough, though, and a large force of islanders attacked a contingent sent ashore for fresh water. Twelve of the crew were killed, and twenty wounded. The inlet was dubbed Massacre Bay.

The ship and its crew were last seen in Botany Bay on 26th January 1788 (the very day of the white settlement of Australia) by the English. At this stage, La Pérouse had planned to set out upon a systematic investigation of the South Sea islands, particularly New Caledonia and the Solomons. Instead, he sailed off enigmatically into maritime history. For several years, the mystery of *La Boussole* exceeded even that of the *Marie Celeste*. Not only had its crew vanished into thin air, but the 500-ton vessel in which they sailed had also performed a neat disappearing trick.

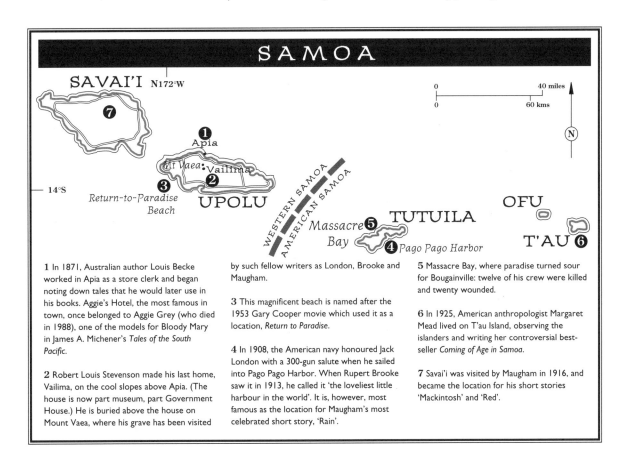

SAMOA

1 In 1871, Australian author Louis Becke worked in Apia as a store clerk and began noting down tales that he would later use in his books. Aggie's Hotel, the most famous in town, once belonged to Aggie Grey (who died in 1988), one of the models for Bloody Mary in James A. Michener's *Tales of the South Pacific*.

2 Robert Louis Stevenson made his last home, Vailima, on the cool slopes above Apia. (The house is now part museum, part Government House.) He is buried above the house on Mount Vaea, where his grave has been visited by such fellow writers as London, Brooke and Maugham.

3 This magnificent beach is named after the 1953 Gary Cooper movie which used it as a location, *Return to Paradise*.

4 In 1908, the American navy honoured Jack London with a 300-gun salute when he sailed into Pago Pago Harbor. When Rupert Brooke saw it in 1913, he called it 'the loveliest little harbour in the world'. It is, however, most famous as the location for Maugham's most celebrated short story, 'Rain'.

5 Massacre Bay, where paradise turned sour for Bougainville: twelve of his crew were killed and twenty wounded.

6 In 1925, American anthropologist Margaret Mead lived on T'au Island, observing the islanders and writing her controversial best-seller *Coming of Age in Samoa*.

7 Savai'i was visited by Maugham in 1916, and became the location for his short stories 'Mackintosh' and 'Red'.

Obereyau Enchantress, *the costume for the queen, by Philippe Jacques de Loutherbourg,*
from the 1785 Covent Garden production of Omai

Needless to say, the disappearance of the expedition came at an inconvenient time in the history of France. Attention was diverted from La Pérouse's long silence by such matters as the taking of the Bastille on 14th July 1789. None the less, an outcry from the scientific fraternity led to the Assembly allocating funds for a South Seas search party. By 1791, the Revolution was in full swing as the 500-ton frigate *La Recherché* set sail under the command of A.R.J. de Bruni, Chevalier d'Entrecasteaux.

La Pérouse's rescuers, however, were subject to their own tragedies. They were visited by scurvy, not to mention a considerable army of weevils and maggots, and a lack of fresh water afflicted them throughout the voyage. Haunted by these curses, they visited Tonga, but found that the trail here was cold. Heading for the Santa Cruz group, in the Solomons, they discovered the previously unmapped and wild island of Vanikoro. Little did they realise, but the trail here was as hot as it would get. With sixty cases of scurvy, however, and a crew made anxious by news of the civil war at home, the ship slunk back to France. The commander himself died of scurvy in July.

It was almost four decades before the riddle was solved. In 1829, the Irish commander Peter Dillon was visiting Vanikoro when he came across an islander proudly sporting a silver sword. He further came to hear about two mysterious European men, now untraceable, who had lived on the island for a while shortly after the disappearance of *La Boussole*. The extraordinary story was pieced together after further enquiries and investigations of the sea floor. It seems that La Pérouse's ship had been wrecked upon the reef of Vanikoro, whereupon he and his crew had built a new boat on the island. This, in turn, was also wrecked upon the reef, but this time, as the crew crawled ashore, they were slaughtered — except, presumably, two lucky survivors. A bronze ship's bell and a crucifix, believed to belong to *La Boussole*, were subsequently retrieved. A memorial to the ship and its star-crossed commander now stands on the south side of the island. Despite some valiant attempts, the era brought forth no other French mariner as august as Bougainville.

Two later Gallic circumnavigations, however, more than compensated for the ill-fated *Boussole*. France had been humiliated by the various colonies that had been taken from her due to her vulnerability at the time of the Revolution so it became a priority to raise the nation's prestige. This was at the beginning of a new period of distant exploration, marked particularly by a series of circumnavigations by the Russians. It was therefore the brainchild of seaman Louis de Freycinet to organise yet another French expedition, and to give it a primarily scientific intent.

In 1817, Freycinet commanded the 350-ton corvette *L'Uraine* (aptly named after the muse for astronomy and geometry) on a three-year voyage which took in such South Sea archipelagoes as the Marianas, Hawaii and Samoa. From this voyage arose six volumes of text and four atlases filled with delicate and unique illustrations — atlases that are still considered models of their kind today. Keeping up the momentum, Louis Isidore Duperrey organised and commanded a second scientific circumnavigation (1822–25) in the 380-ton transport vessel *La Coquille*. Duperrey's major island stopovers were at Tahiti, Bora-Bora, New Ireland and Kosrae, in the Carolines, and from his fieldwork came invaluable geographical, hydrographical, zoological and geological discoveries. Back home, the voyage was dubbed 'scientifically exemplary'.

At around the same time as these great French scientific voyages, Russia undertook five trips to the Pacific, under commanders Adam Ivan von Krusenstern (1803–6), Otto von Kotzebue (1815–18, 1823–26), Fabian Bellingshausen (1819–21) and Fedor Petrovitch Lutke (1826–29). Their purpose was mainly to discover quicker routes for the fur trade from the American north-west and to find the Northwest Passage. Perhaps the most interesting of these — and certainly one of the happiest of early contacts with the islanders — was the first voyage of Kotzebue, in the small two-masted brig *Rurik*. On board, acting as naturalist, was the German poet Adelbert von Chamisso, and artist Louis Choris, who were mainly responsible for promoting the voyage's significance.

By March 1816, they had reached Easter Island, and by the end of April they saw the low-lying atoll of Penrhyn — northernmost of the Cook Islands — with its huge inner lagoon and natives with raised scarifications across their chests. Westwards they sailed to the Gilberts and the Marshalls, then east to California, reaching the Hawaiian island of Oahu by November. Here they met King Kamehameha I, and were taken to his native-style palace, where his queens were languishing upon soft mats and cast lascivious glances at the young Chamisso. Many of the crew attending a spectacular religious ceremony were transfixed by the attractions of the hula, and left the island with tremendous reluctance.

Returning to the Marshalls, they discovered several of the group's unmapped, low-lying, deeply green atolls. For the duration of their stay, Maloelap, with the largest lagoon in the Ratak chain, was their base. They were astonished at the natives because 'their gentleness and generosity made them trust the foreigners who dominated them'. And the friendliest of all those whom Chamisso met was Kadu: 'One of the men I have loved most.' Kadu became intermediary and guide for the Russians as they meandered, spellbound, from island to lovely island within the group. They even cultivated a garden on Maloelap for fresh vegetables, sowing peas, corn and greens, and leaving it in the hands of a delighted Kadu when they left. Setting forth in November 1817, they departed the Pacific via 'green and scented' Guam in the Marianas (later associated more with the stench of cordite, during the fierce battles of World War II).

The ship returned triumphantly to St Petersburg, without even one death. Kotzebue was promoted to captain-lieutenant of the Marine Guards, and eventually undertook another circumnavigation. Chamisso settled in Berlin where he became the first conservator of the Botanical Gardens. He collaborated with Kotzebue in 1821 on their account of the voyage, *Journey Around the World*. In 1829, his reputation as a poet also flourished when he published 'Salas y Gomez', a narrative poem reminiscing about the voyage, written on board the *Rurik*. In 1835, he authored his own *Voyage Journal*, which was highly regarded and extremely popular.

By the mid 1840s, it seemed there was little left to discover other than the fine detail of the globe's great oceans. (That elusive Northwest Passage, however, kept its whereabouts a well-guarded secret until 1850, and its entirety was not discovered until 1903.) When the English vessel *Great Britain* crossed the Atlantic in 1843 with a screw propeller, the great era dominated by Bougainville and Cook came to an end. The enthusiastic, humanitarian spirit of discovery was largely replaced by more materialistic preoccupations. Colonization of the islands followed, with convicts and missionaries leading the way. The peaceful, friendly mood of early visitors became one of force and exploitation. The enchantment of discovery had largely gone; the vision of paradise seemed to be getting a little out of focus.

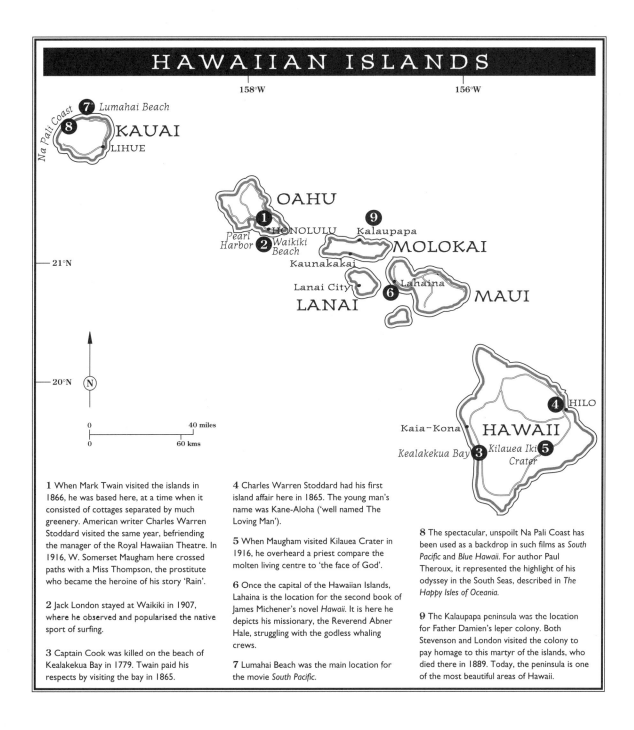

HAWAIIAN ISLANDS

158°W   156°W

Na Pali Coast

7 *Lumahai Beach*

8 KAUAI

•LIHUE

OAHU

1

9

HONOLULU   *Kalaupapa*

2 *Waikiki*   MOLOKAI
Beach

Pearl
Harbor

21°N

Kaunakakai

Lanai City•   •*Lahaina*

LANAI   **6**   MAUI

N

20°N (N)

0   40 miles
0   60 kms

HAWAII

4 •HILO

Kaia-Kona

Kealakekua Bay **3** *Kilauea Iki* **5**
Crater

1 When Mark Twain visited the islands in 1866, he was based here, at a time when it consisted of cottages separated by much greenery. American writer Charles Warren Stoddard visited the same year, befriending the manager of the Royal Hawaiian Theatre. In 1916, W. Somerset Maugham here crossed paths with a Miss Thompson, the prostitute who became the heroine of his story 'Rain'.

2 Jack London stayed at Waikiki in 1907, where he observed and popularised the native sport of surfing.

3 Captain Cook was killed on the beach of Kealakekua Bay in 1779. Twain paid his respects by visiting the bay in 1865.

4 Charles Warren Stoddard had his first island affair here in 1865. The young man's name was Kane-Aloha ('well named The Loving Man').

5 When Maugham visited Kilauea Crater in 1916, he overheard a priest compare the molten living centre to 'the face of God'.

6 Once the capital of the Hawaiian Islands, Lahaina is the location for the second book of James Michener's novel *Hawaii*. It is here he depicts his missionary, the Reverend Abner Hale, struggling with the godless whaling crews.

7 Lumahai Beach was the main location for the movie *South Pacific*.

8 The spectacular, unspoilt Na Pali Coast has been used as a backdrop in such films as *South Pacific* and *Blue Hawaii*. For author Paul Theroux, it represented the highlight of his odyssey in the South Seas, described in *The Happy Isles of Oceania*.

9 The Kalaupapa peninsula was the location for Father Damien's leper colony. Both Stevenson and London visited the colony to pay homage to this martyr of the islands, who died there in 1889. Today, the peninsula is one of the most beautiful areas of Hawaii.

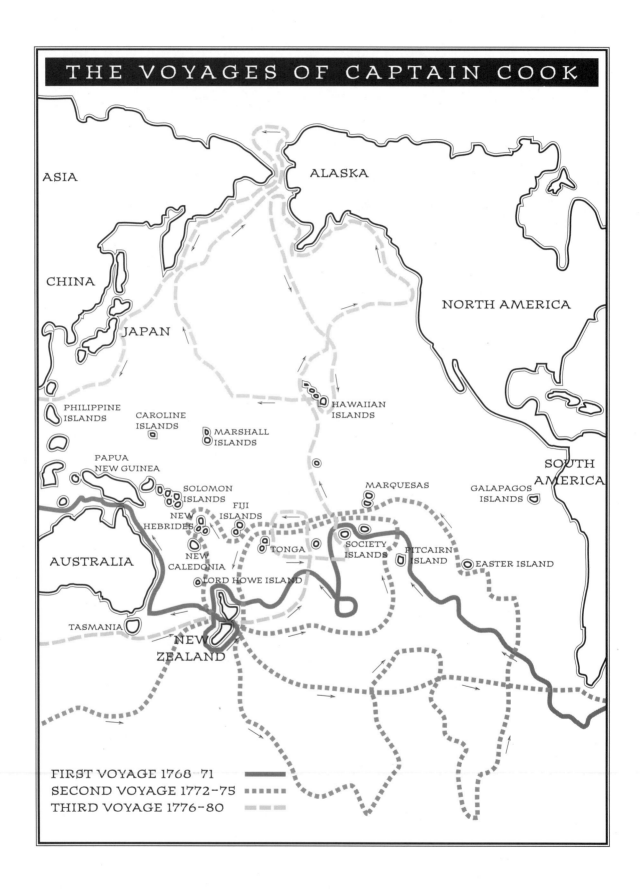

THE VOYAGES OF CAPTAIN COOK

ASIA

ALASKA

CHINA

JAPAN

NORTH AMERICA

PHILIPPINE
ISLANDS

CAROLINE
ISLANDS

MARSHALL
ISLANDS

HAWAIIAN
ISLANDS

SOUTH
AMERICA

PAPUA
NEW GUINEA

SOLOMON
ISLANDS

MARQUESAS

GALAPAGOS
ISLANDS

NEW
HEBRIDES

FIJI
ISLANDS

AUSTRALIA

NEW
CALEDONIA

TONGA

SOCIETY
ISLANDS

PITCAIRN
ISLAND

EASTER ISLAND

LORD HOWE ISLAND

TASMANIA

NEW
ZEALAND

FIRST VOYAGE 1768–71
SECOND VOYAGE 1772–75
THIRD VOYAGE 1776–80

In the Cook Islands, the captain who gave his name to the group is remembered

each time a glass is lifted

Hollywood's recreation of the Bounty *being met by a contingent of Tahitians in Matavai Bay*

The friendly and excited reception of The Resolution and Adventure in Matavai Bay

painted by William Hodges on Cook's second voyage

A rather well-fed and smug-looking Rev. John Williams on Board Ship with Native Implements,
in the South Sea Islands, *painted by Henry Anelay*

CHAPTER TWO

THE MISSIONARY
POSITION

CHRISTIANITY ALONE HAS succeeded in making itself an international religion, and there is no other creed which has not lost some converts to it. 'Go forth to every part of the world, and proclaim the Good News to the whole of creation,' decreed the Gospel of St Mark (16:15), and that is just about what has happened. In more recent times, the spreading of the gospel by such contemporary figures as Billy Graham and the controversial Jimmy Swaggart is often achieved via vast stadiums and satellite TV. But tele-evangelism has not replaced the more traditional face-to-face style once favoured in the depths of an African forest or beneath the palms of a South Sea island.

The connection between missionary work and the phenomenon of colonialism has acquired an unfortunate taint. 'I go back to Africa to make an open path for commerce and Christianity!' announced the great David Livingstone in 1857, rather neatly illustrating the point. And today there is a great deal of money to be made from tele-evangelism in the United States. All of this, however, cannot detract from the nobilty and dedication of various figures in the soul-saving business. Albert Schweitzer's extraordinary work in the heart of French Equatorial Africa, and Mother Teresa's in Calcutta, are, of course, exemplary. Within the field of Oceania, the worthiest of 'God's footsoldiers' were the tragic, selfless Father Damien and the great John Williams.

In 1795, the newly formed London Missionary Society was excited at the prospect of spreading the gospel in the South Seas by members who had read with great interest Cook's

Narrative of his Voyages in the Pacific Ocean. In evangelical circles, the more romantic impressions of the islanders promoted by earlier circumnavigators were being radically modified. This in itself was no bad thing. But the new image, based on reports of bloody wars, isolated infanticide, and even cannibalism, reversed the popular impression of the islander so far in the opposite direction that they now became seen as the distinctly ignoble savage — ugly, debased, pitiable and godless. A favourite illustration, reproduced in many missionary pamphlets of the time, was John Webber's *A Human Sacrifice in Otaheite* (1784). It is easy to see that the old stereotype of the noble savage, despite the sentimental gloss, was in many ways preferable, while the new image justified any amount of 'enlightened' cultural interference. And that lay just around the corner.

On the morning of 10th August 1796, the *Duff*, a 300-ton full-rigged ship purchased by the Society, sailed from London carrying a mission band of four ministers, one surgeon and twenty-five artisans. Great public interest was focussed upon the voyage, with its perceived mix of romantic adventure and divine purpose, and vital contributions of stores, furnishings and equipment were contributed by various merchants and individuals. The enterprise was launched with the goodwill of the government, and veteran seaman Captain James Wilson offered gratis his services as commander.

The fact that most of those who sailed were artisans suggests the conscious cultural dimension of the endeavour. The Society had deemed that, 'Godly men who understand the mechanic arts may be of signal use to this undertaking as missionaries, especially in the South Sea Islands and other uncivilised parts of the world.' It was not just a matter of imposing moral values upon the islanders, but introducing the whole notion of Western civilized progress. On Tahiti, for instance, a printing

As a church is erected on the right of the picture, willing Tahitians throw objects of worship on a fire.
Destruction of the Idols at Otaheite, *from* Missionary Sketches, no. iv, July 1819, *fudges the fact that islanders were mostly bullied into becoming practising Christians*

press was set up, and plans for a sugar factory and the spinning and weaving of cotton were put forward. Under the palm trees and beside the lagoons, the natives would be introduced to the full splendours of those 'dark Satanic mills' back home.

The *Duff* arrived at Tahiti in March 1797, and sailed on to reach Tonga, its other main port of call, in April. On both islands the progress, or otherwise, of the missions was extremely eventful, though any significant breakthroughs were achieved only by the conversion of a usefully prominent chief. From the outset, these English missionaries did their best, as they saw it, to curb violence and immorality, but what they came up against was daunting in the extreme. Most of them, after all, were relatively uneducated craftsmen, with the result that they could only perceive laziness and savagery in a society for which they had little sympathy, understanding or regard.

Matters were hardly helped by the fact that only six of those who originally sailed were married. For the rest of the unfortunate fellowship, life among the Polynesians — one of the most attractive and permissive of races — was nothing short of hellish torture. Several Society members lapsed under the intolerable strain, unable to adhere to the ban on intermarriage. Additionally, it was virtually impossible to instill the Protestant work ethic into a people whose lifestyle was naturally indolent and easygoing. On both islands, the missionaries were also up against seasoned white-skinned sinners: the whalers who turned Tahiti's main port into a 'vortex of iniquity, the Sodom of the Pacific' and the freed Australian convicts on Tonga who incited the natives against the missionaries.

The situation on Tonga was particularly hair-raising, where nine unmarried missionaries were subjected to two and a half years of persecution. At the behest of the convicts, the islanders first stole much of the missionaries' property. One layman sent by the Society soon abandoned the mission in terror to live with the Tongans. Five of the remaining missionaries were one day chased by the islanders, who stole everything they carried with them, then stripped them of their clothes. At the same time, the other three missionaries were also attacked, and these had their brains dashed out. The surviving five buried their comrades, then continued to live on the island in a state of wretchedness and dread, until one day they attracted the attention of a passing ship which rescued them. For the Society it was an inauspicious début on the island, though the second mission established on Tonga had better luck.

The only miracle was how, given such obstacles, and the fact that by 1842 the French had annexed Tahiti, the missionaries gained any foothold at all. In the main, what progress had been made on the two islands was due to the fact that the pre-eminent rulers of both were formally baptized — King Pomare II of Tahiti in 1814, and Chief Haabai of Tonga in 1830. On Tahiti the numbers of those 'saved' was in direct proportion to their fear of the bamboo truncheons wielded by Pomare's police. One attended church or else. With the aid of Pomare, the missionaries were able to enforce an alarming number of prohibitions, other than the obvious one of national forms of religion. These terrible bans included tattooing, national dances, musical instruments, costume, sports, harvest ceremonies — even, surprisingly, the flower garland. As Melville sadly wrote in 1842:

'Doubtless, in thus denationalizing the Tahitians, as it were, the missionaries were prompted by a sincere desire for good, but the effect has been lamentable.'

The crushing effects of the many prohibitions which the missionaries brought to bear upon the Tahitians were alarmingly obvious to such visiting explorers as Fabian Bellingshausen (1820) and Otto von Kotzebue (1823). Bellingshausen was disappointed that the romantic, friendly island Cook had described bore no resemblance to the colourless, subdued place where morality police now poked behind every bush for lurking lovers. Even more vehemently, Kotzebue complained that, 'A religion like this, which forbids every innocent pleasure and cramps or annihilates every mental power, is a libel on the divine founder of Christianity.'

Elsewhere in the Pacific, tales of missionary exploits were equally vivid. The single missionary who landed on Santa Cristina (now Tahuata), in the Marquesas, met with only friendliness and welcome, yet Nature stepped in to terminate the poor man's work. One day, while visiting an American ship in the harbour, a gale drove the vessel so far out to sea that the captain would only drop the missionary off on another island, from which he returned to England in frustration. On the islands of Fiji, the missionaries found themselves particularly unwelcomed by one of the most warlike people in the whole of Oceania. One of the first missionaries there began his work by gathering up and burying the heads, hands and feet of eighty victims of cannibalism. It was only, as elsewhere, when the chief, Thakombau, was baptized in 1854 that conversions became numerous. The most resistant regions, however, were those of the New Hebrides and the Solomons, just as the most amenable islands were those of Samoa. In Samoa, the seeds of Christianity were sown before any missionary had even set foot on the islands. A Samoan who had learned the gospel from Methodists in Tonga spread the word to his own people. The missionary John Williams was to learn a valuable lesson from this Samoan example.

The figure of the South Seas missionary has left an indelible mark upon the literature of the region. Whether as a heroic, isolated, beleaguered victim, or a tenacious, unforgiving zealot, he pops up all over the place. Inevitably, his depiction varies according to the experience and outlook of the writer. Both W. Somerset Maugham and Louis Becke, for example, make no bones about their frank dislike for the fellow. In Becke's neat little tale 'In the Old, Beach-combing Days', the Reverend Gilead Bawl is uncompromising and self-righteous: 'He was a man of nearly six feet in height, with shaven upper lip and white beard, and his eyes, keen, cold and gray, had for the last ten minutes been bent over a copy of the Scriptures, outspread upon his huge knees.' But he is also short-sighted. Because he will not use an unbelieving trader as an intermediary and translator in his negotiations with a chief, he is sent packing from the island of Kosrae in the Carolines. Circumstances, however, wreak a far-reaching revenge upon the population of the island, for the missionaries leave behind them a terrible scourge: measles. Becke presents this as a cruel act of vengeance in keeping with the kind of God a man like Gilead must represent.

One of the most powerful depictions of the South Sea missionary is the awe-inspiring, bullyboy figure of Mr Davidson in Maugham's justly celebrated tale 'Rain'. Davidson's singular appearance is saved for the fifth page of the story: 'He was very tall and thin, with long limbs loosely jointed; hollow cheeks and curiously high cheek-bones; he had so cadaverous an air that it surprised you to notice how full and sensual were his lips.' This wonderful description suggests at once his authority, stern soullessness, and the fatal weakness of carnality. In a sweltering metal-roofed Samoan frame house overhung with coconut palms, the grim missionary succumbs to the voluptuous Miss Sadie Thompson, whom he is attempting to 'save'. His battle against the loose women of the islands actually reflects the war zone of his own soul. Maugham, typically, does not care for either character, because he believed that in the end we all lack dignity in the face of our most basic drives.

Michener has much to say on the subject of missions in the tropics. His tale *Mr Morgan* is set on an isolated Polynesian atoll, where the missionary, Thomas Cobbett, enforces his rule with a rod of iron: 'The pastor knew that his control of Matereva depended upon the absolute loyalty of his wardens, whom he excused of even the most brutal behaviour.' This is not too far from the truth, as we have seen, for the missionaries of Tahiti would rely upon King Pomare's police to fill their churches. None the less, Cobbett is something of a stereotype, and does not so much develop as become thwarted in his ambitions. Far more challenging is the marvellous creation of the Reverend Abner Hale, in Michener's sprawling epic novel *Hawaii*.

Unlike the selection of literary missionaries considered so far, Michener's characters do not exhibit a commanding physical presence. He does not use the cliché of symbolising their strength in a towering frame. Cobbett is 'a small man with watery blue eyes', and Hale is stringy, sallow and small. In this way, Michener makes his footsoldiers more human, and the strength which comes from inside them more awesome. The Reverend Hale is the unlikely hero of such a huge part of the book — entitled 'From the Farm of Bitterness' — that it is really a novel in itself. In this way, Michener gives himself the dramatic advantage of unfolding Abner's character and achievement against the colourful, rousing backdrop of the story of a generation in the history of Hawaii.

From tough, God-fearing Massachusetts farm stock, Abner may be slight of build, but he is dogged and unflinching in what he believes to be right. Not that he is beyond power-dressing for special occasions: regulation black frock coat, stove-pipe hat and a stock. Significantly, Malama, a member of the island aristocracy, comments of Abner that:

> *Of all the white men who have come to Lahaina, he is the only one who has brought more than he took away … He wants me to stop sending men into the forests for sandalwood. He wants me to build better fish ponds and to grow more tarrow. He wants me to protect the girls from the sailors, and to stop baby girls from being buried alive. Everything Makua Hale tells me is a good thing.*

Because Abner develops through time and experience, we gain a fuller picture of the decent missionary on the islands. Obviously, he is seen as part of cultural imperialism, but he is also depicted as part of an attempt to help a dwindling, confused race through a time of great social upheaval. After all, a century after the arrival of the American missionaries, in 1820, more than half the population of the Hawaiian islands was Japanese.

Abner, of course, is a fictional figure, though Michener had several excellent models from which to construct his portrait. One of them, the Belgian missionary Father Damien, born Joseph de Veuster-Wouters (1840–89), also settled in Hawaii, on the island of Molokai. Father Damien is, indeed, one of the most extraordinary missionaries, seen in retrospect as a saintly martyr, but accused at the time as a man who, by sinful behaviour, took unfair advantage of his position.

Damien grew up in a simple, respectable Flemish household in northern Belgium, where he learned some practical carpentry skills and was encouraged to study. He was strong and fit, and his father wanted him to enter business. However, two of his sisters and one brother had entered religious orders, a calling which had also appealed to Damien from the age of eighteen. He went to Louvain, to join the Sacred Heart, or 'Picpus' Fathers, and there heard a talk by a bishop from Hawaii which fired him with enthusiasm for the islands. He set sail in 1863, at the age of twenty-three, and reached the islands in March 1864. At first he settled for a year at Honolulu, capital of Oahu, and then the Big Island of Hawaii for nine years, but eventually felt that he was most needed on Molokai.

In 1865, the government of Hawaii panicked over the spread of the dreadful disease of leprosy, brought to the islands by Chinese migrant workers. (The Hawaiians call the affliction Ma'i Pak, 'Chinese Disease'.) They began a programme of dispatching victims to the most isolated area of the group: the peninsula of Kalaupapa, on the northern coast of Molokai, which is barricaded off from the rest of the island by tall, virtually insurmountable cliffs. Here they imprisoned the unfortunate souls with no facilities other than a few shacks. With no food and no medical aid the place became a notorious hell-hole of dissolution and desperation. Those with the disease struggled to avoid being put ashore as boats pulled in to the island to deliver them. If the ocean was rough, and they could not land easily, the victims were usually thrown overboard to swim to the beach of the peninsula. Those who drowned before reaching the shore were the lucky ones.

Terrified beyond belief, Damien waded through the surf to the peninsula in May 1873, little realising at the time that he would remain here until his death from leprosy sixteen years later. The lepers regarded him suspiciously at first, but he greeted them in Kanaka (few visitors bothered to learn their language), showed no sign of disgust at their often gross disfigurement, and began to fill in holes in the walls of the small chapel of St Philomena. In his very personable way, he won them over. One brought him fruit on a leaf, another a spray of flowers. He slept that night under a pandanus tree, as there was nowhere else.

But Damien was no meek and mild saviour. He was young and strong, and early on realized that he would have to assert himself if he hoped to take the leper colony in hand. He faced up to bullies, rescued children used as slaves, and broke up gambling rings and circles of drunks. Still of his time, he also forbade the practices of the kahunas (medicine men), the observation of native rituals, and in general outlawed non-Christian worship. As much as he grew to love his charges, to him they

The leper colony of Kalaupapa, Molokai, late last century. The sheer mountains virtually cut it off from the rest of the island

were still savages and heathens. However, Damien brought back hope and self-respect to a group whom the Hawaiian authorities had turned their backs upon. He helped them build houses, sow sweet potato, plant flowers, requested a bell for the chapel, nursed them, buried them — even, went the rumours, slept with them. His only relief was that he was fit enough sometimes to struggle up a dangerous cliff path to wander about the rest of the island in peace.

Father Damien was not a name the islands could ignore, for better or for worse. The newspapers on Oahu and the Big Island were filled with articles on his good work, and served to focus sympathy on the community. Collections of food and clothes were organised, and Queen Kapiolani visited the peninsula, promoting the cause even further afield. Nevertheless, within a world that one would have believed to be immune to such things, jealousy over Damien's fame and achievements sprang up within the Church. Even his own Brothers on the other islands became outraged, and the Protestant missionaries, who had themselves forcibly ejected various Catholic footsoldiers from Hawaii, circulated the rumour that the leprosy Damien contracted in 1883 was through sinful practices with the female members of the community.

In June 1889, two months after Damien's death, Robert Louis Stevenson visited the leper colony and lived there for eight days. He was deeply moved, sometimes to tears. He had heard that Damien was 'a European peasant, dirty, bigoted, untruthful, unwise, tricky, but superb with generosity'. Yet when he read a letter in a Church journal from the Reverend C.M. Hyde of Honolulu, running Damien down as coarse and having achieved little good, Stevenson sprang to the defence of the maligned missionary. In an 'Open Letter to the Reverend Hyde of Honolulu', which was published at great legal risk, he accused the man of hypocrisy in damning someone else where he had failed to raise a finger himself. Hyde, Stevenson said, was merely taking cheap shots from the easy comfort of his ivory tower on the Big Island, while Damien had selflessly rolled up his sleeves to help the afflicted and marginalized.

History has been kind to Damien, not the Reverend Hyde. His body was returned to Belgium in 1936, the same year as the process of beatification had begun to make him a saint. His Molokai community still exists, although the number of sufferers are few since the drug Dapsone

Father Damien, disfigured by leprosy, in 1889

was first used for leprosy in 1948. The high regard in which he is still held is reflected in the simple fact that Damien's statue outside the Parliament building of Honolulu is always covered in fresh garlands of bright flowers.

The most celebrated missionary of Oceania is certainly John Williams (1796–1839). Born in Middlesex in England, he was given a commercial education in ironmongery, at which he excelled. His parents, however, were strict Congregationalists, and John joined the Tabernacle in Moorfields, where he took an active role. The Tabernacle closely followed the work of the London Missionary Society, and Williams determined to offer himself to them as a field worker. After passing exams in November 1816, the Society sent him and his wife to the Pacific on the *Harriet*, where they travelled via Australia to Eimeo (now Moorea), Tahiti's smaller sister island. With him were two other missionaries — John Muggeridge Orsmond and William Ellis — and their wives.

By the time they arrived, a church had been established on Moorea and, on Tahiti, King Pomare II had been baptized. In this relatively stable period, Williams and his companions remained on Eimeo, assisting the mission station and learning the Polynesian language. In 1808, however, after the death of the old king, Pomare II had experienced political opposition to his sovereignty from rebel chiefs. At one point, he had fled to Eimeo, where some of the missionaries from Tahiti had also taken shelter. Back on the mainland, the rebels, in a rather neat symbolic gesture, had melted down the type from the mission presses and turned the metal into bullets.

An ambitious and shrewd young man, Pomare had seen the way ahead: an alliance with the Church, not to mention the power of learning the English language, could help establish him as ruler. In 1814, he was baptized in grand style before thousands of his subjects, and it was a turning point for Christianity in Polynesia and for the young king's future. Following this, the chiefs from the nearby Society Islands, who had assisted Pomare regain supreme rule of his people, visited Eimeo and asked the three new missionaries to help establish the Church on their own islands. For this reason, in June 1818, Williams, Ellis and Muggeridge Orsmond landed at the island of Huahine to a jubilant welcome. Indeed, their arrival had drawn huge crowds from all the neighbouring islands. Amongst the throng was Tamatoa, the king of Raiatea, who enthusiastically claimed Williams as his very own missionary.

Williams thus parted company with his two partners in 1818, settling on Raiatea with sufficient knowledge of Polynesian to enable him to preach to the islanders. He became aware, however, that learning the language of one's charges was only half the battle. Williams always took a lively and sympathetic interest in the culture and everyday lives of the islanders wherever he went. This alone set him apart from the great body of missionaries in the field of the Pacific, and explains the cordiality of his reception wherever he went in Polynesia.

He came to see that his work on Raiatea was hampered by a social structure barely noticed by earlier Society field-workers. On the islands, social systems did not demand the formation of centres after the European fashion of villages and towns. In the main, tiny settlements, usually consisting of family dwellings, were scattered haphazardly inland or adjacent to the lagoon. This peaceful solitude was one of the delights of island life noted by some visitors only when it began to disappear. Towns and villages are the consequence of more commercially based societies. Williams, however, needed more community spirit to take control, and induced the islanders to form a common settlement around a chapel and schoolhouse. Here is a clear example of spiritual ambitions and the dictates of Western progress working hand in hand.

Like many another missionary in the South Seas, Williams felt impelled to declare war on native 'indolence'. He began by building a house on the English model, hoping it would serve as an example to his flock, and stimulate them to follow his labour. The fact that native dwellings were often beautiful and uniquely suited to the climate did not occur to Williams any more than it did to other representatives of 'civilization'. The later introduction of corrugated iron sheets, now largely adopted as roofing for island homes, must represent the reductio ad absurdum of this policy for improvement.

In 1819, Williams introduced a complete code of laws, adopted by popular vote, which included trial by jury. This system was the first of its kind within Polynesia. The same year, he introduced sugar cane to the island, and opened the mill by turning the rollers, which he had made himself by hand. Misplaced or otherwise, Williams's industry was boundless, and his relatively empathetic relationship with his charges realized astonishing successes. Maybe in part because of all this good fortune, he began to hatch plans of an imposing ambition. At one point, he even planned to sever his connection with the Society and take off into the islands as the fancy took him. But his dreams, grand as they were, would remain usefully within the parameter of his missionary work.

The Society did not in general approve of Williams taking the reins into his own hands, but he was able to carve out a course of his own by dint of some inherited wealth. In his own words, Williams's ambitions could not be contained 'within the narrow limits of a single reef'. In 1821, he travelled to Sydney, where he purchased a 90-ton schooner, the *Endeavour*. In 1822, he set off on what was to be an epic series of voyages to most significant islands in the Polynesian region. And whichever atoll or mountainous island at which he dropped anchor — from the Cooks to the Australs — he was the first to understand that the successful evangelizing of the South Seas must eventually be undertaken by Christians of the native races. Williams therefore left in his wake a whole series of Polynesian missionaries, confident that the islanders were far more susceptible to persuasion by their own kind.

When, at last, the *Endeavour* proved too costly to keep afloat, again using his own initiative, Williams decided to build his own seaworthy vessel — and a colourful chapter in the history of the South Pacific was born. Returning to Raiatea, with marvellous ingenuity, Williams made creative use of what materials were available, learning much more about native traditions along the way. In lieu of a saw, the trees were split with wedges, and a bellows was constructed from goatskin. Rope was made from the bark of the hibiscus, sails from native matting, joints were packed with coconut husk, a rudder fashioned from a large hoe and an anchor made of stone. In fifteen weeks, the vessel was completed, a ship of 60 feet (18 metres) in length and 18 feet (5.5 metres) in width, which was named the *Messenger of Peace.*

This was the first vessel to represent the Society within the Pacific, though there were to be several more. When the first ran aground in 1864, it was replaced by a second ship (hereafter they were all named *John Williams*), which was itself wrecked a year later. By 1868, a third *John Williams* was launched, which was pensioned off in 1893 in favour of a steamer. It was this ship that was immortalized in Arthur Grimble's book, *A Pattern of Islands*, when he saw it in the Gilberts in 1916. In all, there were to be six ships named after Williams, and they were a familiar sight throughout the Pacific until the 1950s.

By 1834, Williams could truthfully report that, 'No group of islands, nor single island of importance, within 2,000 miles of Tahiti had been left unvisited.' That year, he visited England, and was lionized by authorities and the general public alike. He had star status at numerous meetings, where the stories of his adventures quickened the hearts and imaginations of those who had gathered to hear him. In April 1837, he published the concisely titled *A Narrative of Missionary Enterprise in the South Sea Islands, with Remarks on the Natural History of the Islands, Origin, Languages, Traditions, and Usages of the Inhabitants.* It ran into several reprints, exciting the attention of the general reading public, scientists and those interested in Williams's calling. But his head was not turned by all this high-powered publicity. When the islands called, he had to obey. Later that month, he set sail again with great excitement.

On this final leg of his Oceanic odyssey, Williams visited Samoa, Tahiti and the New Hebrides. The latter — his first and last stab at travelling to regions beyond Polynesia — proved to be his undoing. At Dillon's Bay, on Erromanga, he was killed and eaten by natives who had previously been mistreated by the crew of an English ship dealing in sandalwood. As news of the Reverend's death travelled from island to island across the length and breadth of Polynesia, heartfelt cries went up of, 'Oh, my father! My father! Williamu!' A stone at Apia, in Western Samoa, marks the place where his collected remains were buried. The fact that Williams died very much in the manner of the great Captain Cook served to enhance the significance of his death back home. Williams became something of a martyr, and his transfiguration increased the numbers wishing to follow his example into the field.

A highly melodramatic impression of John Williams Clubbed to Death on Erromanga, *1839*

The Reverend John Williams is one of the most vivid figures in the history of the Pacific, combining roistering exploits with extraordinary religious zeal. There is, however, one other larger-than-life missionary figure of Polynesia — though his achievements are less clear-cut than those of Williams, and his zeal a little less religious. Indeed, the American preacher Walter Murray Gibson (1822–88) fits quite snugly into the notorious pages of Michener's set of non-fiction essays, *Rascals in Paradise.*

If Williams seemed to accept physical challenge as a part of his missionary work for Polynesia, Gibson positively thrived upon flamboyant daredevilry. If Williams seemed ambitious, Gibson's aspirations were on the scale of Cecil B. De Mille's. The focus of Gibson's career seemed nothing less than the uniting of the whole Pacific into one empire under the aegis of Hawaii — with himself, of course, in a principal role.

Significantly, Gibson was born upon a stormy sea, in the Bay of Biscay. He was the third son of English emigrants, bidding farewell to Northumberland for the dream of the United States. Early on, he was inspired by tales of Sumatra brought back by an adventure-loving uncle, and instilled with a sense of daring by growing up in the wild backwoods of South Carolina. As a young man he became involved in exploits as varied as the California gold rush and the smuggling of arms to Guatemala.

Gibson's biggest adventure, however, began with his religious conversion and, like everything else in his life, this was achieved in no modest fashion. In 1859, he was in Salt Lake City talking to Brigham Young, the great Mormon leader, attempting to convince the man to establish a Mormon settlement in the South Seas. Brother Young suggested instead that Gibson's enthusiasm might be best harnessed as a missionary, spreading the Mormon cause throughout the Pacific. After a little thought, Gibson decided he liked such lofty schemes, and a year later was converted.

On 4th July 1861, he landed at Honolulu. From here, he travelled to Maui, then, eventually, took a native whaleboat to Lanai. Here, at last, he discovered an operation in keeping with his own grandiose designs. On this island, the Mormon Church was establishing a spectacular City of Joseph (after the Mormon prophet Joseph Smith) on a 5,000-acre (2,023-hectare) plot of land purchased in 1853. 'I will plant my stakes here,' Gibson majestically announced, 'and make a home for the rest of my days.' In no time he was head of an agricultural colony at Palawai, and took on the imposing title of Chief President of the Isles of the Sea. Gibson

Missionary Home and Environs in the Island of Otaheite *by W. Wilson, 1799.*
As Tahitians prepare to disrobe and bathe on the left of the picture, on the right the
missionary families staunchly set out to impose their culture

believed he was establishing the New Jerusalem in the land of 'the red-skinned children of Abraham'.

The children of Abraham, for their part, donated livestock and cash to the Church, and Brother Gibson, rather shadily, sold off posts within the mission to build up finances. Slowly, the old, entrepreneurial Gibson reasserted himself as profit and power took first place before the planning of utopia. When a drought and plague of insects threatened the crops, rather like the ruthless hero of a Charlton Heston movie, he worked the islanders like slave labour to save what he could. Rumours also arose that Gibson had sequestered funds to purchase half of the island, and that all Church property on Lanai was now in his name. There were voices raised among his native followers and, in April 1862, a delegation from Salt Lake City arrived to investigate.

Gibson was excommunicated from the Mormon Church, and the New Jerusalem was, with great embarrassment, relocated to Oahu, where a temple stands today in the midst of the community's sugar-cane fields. Gibson stayed on in Lanai, however, enjoying his ill-gotten gains, and watching his own personal Utopia of island estates flourish under the sun. There was still the tone of an biblical prophet about him: 'I would fill this lovely crater with corn and wine and oil and babies and love and health and brotherly rejoicing and sisterly kisses and the memories of me for evermore.'

Not even those sisterly kisses, to which he was very partial, could hold him for long in a static utopia. In 1872, he moved to Honolulu to enter politics — a small step, for him, from the pulpit. Here, Gibson used his considerable experience of the Hawaiian language and customs to gain him popularity at the polls, happy to jump on the convenient political bandwagon of 'Hawaii for the Hawaiians!' to increase his influence. Typically, as with his farming exploits on Lanai, he often did good at the same time as boosting his self-aggrandisement — a fact that makes it difficult to condemn him as wholly black-hearted. Indeed, even his wild-seeming scheme for a Pacific empire has, to some extent, come about with today's South Pacific Commission. Sexual

In Robert Smirke's Cession of Matavai, *1798, the Tahitians bow low to the superiority of gracefully attired missionaries and their families*

scandals and more sequestering of funds ensured his downfall, however, and he was forced to leave Hawaii in 1887.

Today, Gibson enjoys a reputation which owes more to impetuousness than to evil. He has inveigled his way into the pages of Robert Louis Stevenson, and even appears in Nathaniel Hawthorne's popular book of reflections, *Our Old Home*. Having himself met this most unlikely of missionaries, Hawthorne had to admit that Gibson was 'a gentleman of refined manner, handsome figure, and remarkably intellectual aspect'.

There are now more of God's footsoldiers in the field than ever, although the heyday of the missionary's adulation has come and gone. In the late eighteenth century, and throughout the nineteenth, the missionary was perceived as a romantic hero and exemplar — a celebrity on a par with today's sports or media personalities. They would return home to headline news, nation-wide tours and enthusiastic crowds. Books and magazines promoted an appealing image of suffering, bravery and, ultimately, nobility in the face of heathen savagery. Increasingly, however, the link between cultural imperialism and missionary work served to tarnish this vision. There are many countries, notably those of the Muslim world, which have closed their doors firmly on the missionary. Today, soul-saving has returned, ironically, to the birthplace of the missionary movement: Europe itself is now seen as the new 'Dark Continent'.

One of the most celebrated images brought back from any of Cook's voyages is John Webber's A Human Sacrifice in Otaheite.
The stark horror is increased considerably by having the figure of Cook himself observing the ceremony

CHAPTER THREE

PAINTING

PARADISE

OCEANIA OFFERS THE artist a wonderful palette of colours — from the floral to the aquatic — all of which are defined by the sharp, clear quality of the light. It is this light, more than anything, that has delighted and inspired the painter and the photographer. What has fascinated the Western art lover, though, are images of an easy-going, sensual paradise quite at odds with the greyer realities of life back home. Inevitably, one links the region with Gauguin, yet while he is indeed the area's paramount visiting artist, others have tackled the richness of the Oceanic human and physical environment with far greater range and detail.

The odd thing is how few artists have visited the region. When one thinks that five major writers travelled to Oceania before the turn of this century, and at least half a dozen since, it is strange that only three major prominent artists have ventured to the South Seas under their own steam. Many nineteenth-century artists shared Gauguin's disenchantment with what they perceived as a 'corrupt' Western civilization, but few saw the need to travel far to escape it. Many were content to search for simplicity and innocence either within their own imaginations, or by returning to nature closer to home.

During the period since 1890, John La Farge, Paul Gauguin and Henri Matisse were each to make self-supported journeys to the South Seas. The earliest artists to enter the South Pacific, however, did so as part of the bag and baggage of circumnavigation. And along with their paints, canvases, easels, pencils and sketchbooks, they brought with them the same romantic nostalgia as the rest of their crews. The current fashion was for the ancient classical civilizations of the Greek and Roman world. The objectivity they brought to bear upon plants and animals was not as evident, therefore, in their attitude towards the islanders and landscapes.

The subject of these artistic styles caused some controversy at the time. Father and son naturalists Johann and George Forster, who sailed with Cook's second voyage, were the most vocal of the objectors: 'The plates which ornamented the history of Captain Cook's former voyage, have been justly criticised, because they exhibited to our eyes the pleasing forms of antique figures and draperies, instead of those Indians of which we wished to form some idea.' And it was certainly the craft of the eighteenth-century engraver, rather than the interpretation of the original artists, which was to blame for this classical idealisation of South Sea life. Yet, perhaps 'blame' is hardly an appropriate word, as there was at the time no systematic discipline for studying human society, and the unknown was inevitably seen in terms of the known. However, despite a tendency to gild Polynesian society and landscapes here and there, these illustrations still conveyed much of ethnographic interest, and certainly conveyed the astonishment and reverence of the early visitors to a 'pre-fallen' Oceania.

Of all these artist–explorers, by far the most influential were those who accompanied Cook. This was mainly due to the shrewd general planning of these voyages, but also because these young artists went gloriously beyond the limits of their briefs. The Admiralty had instructed them 'to give a more perfect Idea thereof than can be formed by written descriptions only'. It was their job to supply three main classes of graphic record: 'scenes from savage life', natural history subjects and 'views' (by which was meant mainly coastline profiles to complement cartographic records). Each young man, however, found the time to break the straightjacket of his orders, driven by the mystery, eroticism and vibrant colours of this strange new world.

On board the *Endeavour* was twenty-three-year-old Sydney Parkinson (1745–71), the son of an Edinburgh brewer, who was hired as a natural history draughtsman at a salary of £80 a year. Following the death by illness of second draughtsman Alexander Buchan, Parkinson also took over landscapes and 'scenes from savage life', both of which he handled well. Cook was full of praise for this amiable young man, and Banks spoke of his 'unbounded industry' in producing a larger body of work than was expected. He would frequently sit up working all night.

Parkinson quickly made friends with the islanders. Indeed, all the artist–explorers were to do so, largely due to the fact that they wielded a paintbrush, not a gun. Being a Scottish Quaker, though, Parkinson disapproved of intimate relations with the natives, and kept his friendships on an innocent basis. He wandered freely among the Tahitians sketching and painting. He discovered the need for a rather stuffy mosquito-net frame placed about him while he worked, for the flies were not only a constant bother, but they actually ate the paint straight off the canvas. He was more interested in landscapes and everyday native life than was Banks, his mentor, and frequently used his own time and initiative to record these things.

Tahiti Revisited *by William Hodges. Beautiful, unspoilt landscape,*
a lifestyle of leisure spent close to nature and the lack of inhibitions in the bathing Tahitian women seemed
to sum up the kind of utopia Europeans believed Polynesia to be

One of Louis Choris's elegant, stylized depictions of the South Seas, Landscape
of the Ratak Islands

John La Farge's Military Dance in Samoa, *one of his many graceful, light and airy depictions
of traditional South Sea choreography*

Gauguin did not always paint Polynesian women as squat, as in the celebratory Two Tahitian Women

Polynesia, the Sky *by Matisse, is one of several 'cut-outs', abstract designs made from coloured paper shapes*

Astonishingly, Parkinson was the only person to comment on the beauty of Tahiti's Matavai
Bay, with its backdrop of steep verdant hills, as they first entered it on the morning of 13th April 1769:
'The land appeared as uneven as a piece of crumpled paper, being divided irregularly into hills and
valleys; but a beautiful verdure covered both, even to the tops of the highest peaks.' His wash drawing,
View of the Peaks of Orowhaina [Orohena] in the Bay of Matavai, was made on the spot — the product
of a gut reaction to fabulous beauty, rather than the more analytic response required for a scientific
record. As his sojourn in Polynesia lengthened, the extraordinary situation in which he found himself
began to work on his imagination: he responded more and more to conditions of weather, light and
atmosphere. His work reveals a growing sensitivity to tropical storms, the sun breaking through
clouds, birds flying before a rain shower. In the Tuamotus, he was transfixed by the colours in the
lagoon: 'The water within the Reefs ... seagreen ... brownish towards the edge of the Reefs, the
Breakers white ... this stript and streakt with a dark colour of a purple cast occasion'd by the
intervention of clouds between the sun and water.' This developing passion was quite over and above
the more pragmatic dictates of his formal instructions.

Back home, Parkinson's mysterious and brooding depictions of the marae (Tahitian places of
worship) stirred public interest beyond any of his other depictions of island life. There is about these
drawings a sense of loneliness and solemnity, which was interpreted by Evangelists as savage and by
the thoughtful as arcadian exotica.

Parkinson died at sea of malaria on 26th January 1771. His *Journal* appeared in 1773 in
considerable numbers, and was enthusiastically received. (A second edition appeared in 1784.) The
Gentleman's Magazine in particular gave it a glowing reception. It contained a portrait of the artist
by James Newton, and had twenty-three plates from Parkinson's drawings to accompany the text.
With Parkinson, it is certainly more the engraver's hand than the original works which display any
classical refinements.

The main artist on Cook's second voyage was twenty-eight-year-old London-born William
Hodges (1744–97), who was employed on the recommendation of Lord Palmerston as a landscape
and figure artist. (He was not, however, the first choice. That had been a Thomas Jones, but his
mother had forbidden him to go!) With Hodges, there is a clearer division between picturesque
landscape and practical coastal views and he was not above rearranging details for pleasing effect.
Notwithstanding this, he sometimes painted straight from the scene before him, so confident was he
with the brush. This factor accounts for the freshness and detail of various canvases. He also became
even more concerned than Parkinson with the problems of light and colour, and was certainly rather
less concerned with ethnographic interest. He worked so intensively that it is believed that he ran out
of oil paints by September 1773.

Again, Hodges was popular with the islanders. On Tahiti, they would carry around his
portfolio for him, and were amused and delighted by their drawn or painted likenesses. He was thus
in a position to achieve a splendid portrait of Tu, the founder of the great Pomare dynasty. The
'classical' style of some paintings — for example, the posed figures in elegant draperies — seem as

much his response to the islanders' natural grace, as an attempt to depict arcadia. As for his portraits, they are the first depictions of Pacific islanders which treat the subjects as individuals rather than ethnographic samples. In all areas, Hodges attempted to rise above stereotyped conceptions. 'Everything has a particular character,' he wrote, 'and certainly it is the finding out of the real and natural character which is required.'

Upon his return to England, the Royal Academy exhibited two of Hodges' paintings of Tahiti in 1776, to great public interest. Those who saw them were particularly enthralled by *A View Taken in the Bay of Otaheite Peha (Vaitepiha)*. Set against a lovely glowing landscape, in the foreground are two young female Tahitian bathers. To the public of the time, such a vision affirmed their image of the South Seas as a place of contented languor and ingenuous eroticism. It is very apparently not an 'official' depiction of the island, but one inspired by the young man's direct, candid response to the spirit of an earlier Polynesia. It is also, very obviously, a landscape free from any signs of European presence, and this peaceful, untouched quality has been taken as a political statement by the young artist. The painting's overall impact was not lost upon those who filed through the Academy for a glimpse of it.

The graphics team for Cook's final voyage was spearheaded by the twenty-four-year-old John Webber (1752–93). Webber was the son of a Swiss sculptor who settled in England, and was employed by Dr Solander (the naturalist who had accompanied Cook on his first voyage) for his portraiture and landscapes. From the very beginning, he was seen as providing an official visual record of the voyage in a way which Parkinson and Hodges had not been. Even before they sailed, he was also chosen by Cook to be the illustrator of his account of the voyage. Webber was, therefore, less fanciful in his style than the other two painters.

Webber was still subject to his own angle on matters, though. For example, his human figures on the whole omit individual characteristics. There is no corpulence or deformity in paradise, merely a statuesque quality in the classical mode. Also, the eternal bachelor, Webber did few portraits of native women. Yet, oddly enough, he did paint one of the most celebrated images of the Polynesian female.

Poedua, the daughter of a chief of Raiatea, was described in the ship's log of the second voyage as, 'a young Lady about 15 years of age, of middleing stature, rather slender, and Delicate, with good Teeth and Eyes and a regular set of features, Black Hair and her complexion so fair that I have seen many Ladies in England much more of a Brunett'. For Webber's body of work, she is uncharacteristically erotic, with an almost Mona Lisa smile, jasmine in her shoulder-length hair, bare breasts, generous hips and delicately positioned arms (*see page 20*). This was the first of Webber's pictures to be displayed at the Royal Academy, and aroused tremendous excitement and curiosity. Together with Hodges' very popular bathers, this canvas did much to create an impression of the South Seas as an erotic paradise.

On his return, Webber was asked to display 200 of his paintings at Windsor Castle, the King's country retreat. The drawing entitled *A Human Sacrifice at Otaheite* raised as much interest as the startling portrait of Poedua. Although most of Webber's work portrayed the sublimity of Polynesia, this image of a human sacrifice, rather unfortunately, stirred up a public eager, after Cook's death, to believe in Polynesian barbarity. On a quite different note, Webber also provided, in the Hawaiian painting *A View of Kealakekua Bay*, probably the first depiction of someone surfing (perhaps the earliest written description being by Mark Twain). In later years, his many exhibitions at the Academy always carefully avoided the thorny subject of Hawaii and Cook's death, and he became quite wealthy and popular from his idyllic series 'Views of the South Seas'. Many of these were reproduced in books, and sold well for over thirty-five years. In 1791, Webber was elected a full member of the Royal Academy.

It would be impossible to list here all the artists who accompanied the explorers to the South Pacific, though so many performed outstanding work in their fashion. Not the least of the remainder was the Russian, Louis Choris (1795–1828), who travelled

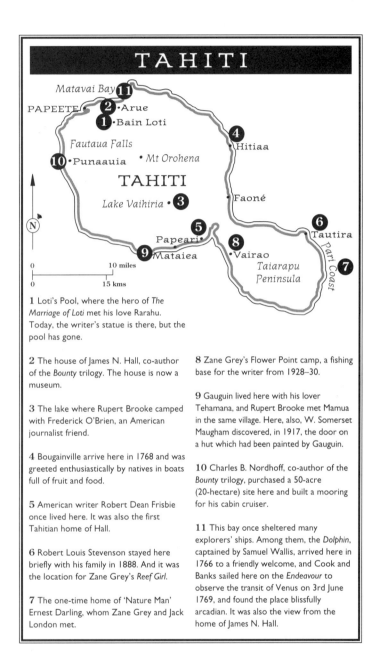

TAHITI

1 Loti's Pool, where the hero of *The Marriage of Loti* met his love Rarahu. Today, the writer's statue is there, but the pool has gone.

2 The house of James N. Hall, co-author of the *Bounty* trilogy. The house is now a museum.

3 The lake where Rupert Brooke camped with Frederick O'Brien, an American journalist friend.

4 Bougainville arrive here in 1768 and was greeted enthusiastically by natives in boats full of fruit and food.

5 American writer Robert Dean Frisbie once lived here. It was also the first Tahitian home of Hall.

6 Robert Louis Stevenson stayed here briefly with his family in 1888. And it was the location for Zane Grey's *Reef Girl*.

7 The one-time home of 'Nature Man' Ernest Darling, whom Zane Grey and Jack London met.

8 Zane Grey's Flower Point camp, a fishing base for the writer from 1928–30.

9 Gauguin lived here with his lover Tehamana, and Rupert Brooke met Mamua in the same village. Here, also, W. Somerset Maugham discovered, in 1917, the door on a hut which had been painted by Gauguin.

10 Charles B. Nordhoff, co-author of the *Bounty* trilogy, purchased a 50-acre (20-hectare) site here and built a mooring for his cabin cruiser.

11 This bay once sheltered many explorers' ships. Among them, the *Dolphin*, captained by Samuel Wallis, arrived here in 1766 to a friendly welcome, and Cook and Banks sailed here on the *Endeavour* to observe the transit of Venus on 3rd June 1769, and found the place blissfully arcadian. It was also the view from the home of James N. Hall.

with the poet and naturalist Adelbert von Chamisso on the voyage of the *Rurik* (1815–18). They visited various areas of the South Seas, though Hawaii was the only Polynesian destination. Choris undertook a great many sketches, mainly of the ethnographic and natural history variety, though some featured islanders and landscapes. The accuracy and delicacy of these made them very popular, especially in artistic circles, on his return to Paris. He therefore spent several years in the capital preparing engravings from the drawings, which were published to great acclaim in 1822, with text by Chamisso. In retrospect, his human figures are generally considered too stylised to depict the islanders accurately, though his natural history work is exemplary and very beautiful.

French general and draughtsman Louis-Francois Lejeune (1775–1848) travelled under Commander Louis Isidore Duperrey on the *Coquille* (1822–25), on a course which mainly zigzagged through Polynesia. Lejeune is interesting for his humorously exotic depiction of Tahitian dress of the period, which was beginning to mix items of Western wear with traditional costume. Of particular note is the elegantly colourful *Tahitian Costumes* and the wash drawing *King Pomare III's Guard*. The latter startlingly revealed the decline of a race through the portrayal of three Tahitian soldiers grotesquely half-dressed in cast-off European military uniform. Commander Duperrey wrote how the Tahitians did not even stir themselves to greet the ship. 'The island of Tahiti is now so different from what it was in Cook's time that it is impossible to give you a complete picture of it,' he noted. 'The missionaries of London's Royal Society have totally changed the mores and customs of these people. The women are extraordinarily reserved.' Lejeune's work, which captured images of the islands in transition, illustrated several volumes of Duperrey's account of the voyage, the first of which appeared the year of the *Coquille*'s return.

In a sense, perhaps the Frenchman Louis Julien Viaud (1850–1923) was the last of the artist–explorers. As a midshipman, he sailed to the South Pacific in 1871 in the frigate *Flore*, a flagship bound for Tahiti. But he was no official naturalist or artist. He undertook to study and sketch the flora, fauna, landscapes and people of the islands, but only because they interested him. He was purely a self-taught artist — he began in the nursery with a paintbox — but decided to utilize his talent to illustrate various articles which he sent back home to be published in periodicals such as *Illustration* and *Le Tout du Monde*. At the time, photography was still in its infancy, and his sketches of these exotic outposts were seen as rare and fascinating.

Viaud was an above-average draughtsman, and had a good eye for the moody and picturesque side of the South Seas. On the Marquesas, for instance, he sketched the haughty fallen Queen Vaekehu, forever staring into space — for all the world like one of the Easter Island statues, another of the artist's subjects. On Tahiti, where he fell in love, Viaud was nicknamed 'Loti' (because the islanders had trouble pronouncing any of his names; it is the name of a flower) and sketched the hypnotic, smoky descent of the Fautaua Falls, at the foot of which he first met his love, Rarahu. Viaud's sketches, articles and eventually his novel, *The Marriage of Loti* (1881), fanned the flames of romance until they roared. It is said that Gauguin was moved to visit Tahiti by the spell cast upon him by Viaud — and his sketches were no small part of this magic.

Before Gauguin came to see what 'Loti' had sketched and written about, another major artist arrived in the South Seas. John La Farge (1835–1910) was an American of French extraction who had also read Viaud, as well as Melville, and had even, at six, been moved by *Robinson Crusoe*. La Farge was a strikingly old-world figure — tall, pale, always attired in black, well-read, suave and gracious. He had already made a name for himself, both in his own country and Europe, for his distinguished landscapes, church murals and stained glass work. He was a restless character, always attracted to exotic cultures, and when the pressures of work and family became too great for him in 1890, he swiftly fled to the Pacific. His main ports of call were Hawaii, Fiji, Tonga, Samoa and Tahiti, and he

One of Pierre Loti's delicate sketches, The District of Afareaitu,
the Island of Moorea

was accompanied by his friend, the historian Henry Adams. He wrote that they felt 'like two schoolboys on a lark'.

Like many another visitor, La Farge felt indifferently about Hawaii, finding it neither one thing nor the other. Samoa, however, astonished and excited him as nowhere else had. On the island of Tutuila, where he stayed, he believed he had been transported on a magic carpet to ancient Greece: 'The muscles of the younger men softened and passed into one another as in the modelling of a Greek statue.' He marvelled at their wonderful physiques, the tappa (beaten bark) cloths which seemed so like togas, the beauty of the young women with flowers in their hair, and the simple, elegant dances — and all this within a rustic, arcadian setting.

Immediately he began to sketch, paint and keep a notebook. His own particular style, which looked forward to the Impressionists, was a delicate blending of East and West, of modern techniques together with the classicism that had influenced the earlier artist–explorers. Yet, despite the apparent romanticism of his vision, La Farge was always well versed in island traditions, painting what he saw with accuracy and ethnographic detail. He particularly favoured the human form, especially when in motion, engaged in dance — a style, he noted, 'which might not have been misplaced far back in some classical antiquity'. One could almost say that La Farge's great contribution was in painting and sketching various forms of the Polynesian dance, one of the jewels in the crown of the South Pacific.

The paintings themselves reveal his subtle use of colour and light, based on his own work with prisms.

At the islands' capital of Apia, he met Stevenson, whom he found too self-consciously bohemian. Nevertheless, he followed the writer's advice and went next to Tahiti. He was, on the whole, disappointed by this island, but consoled himself by moving from the centre out to Tautira in the south. Here he was welcomed by Stevenson's friend, the chief, Ori-a-Ori, who came to respect this American gentleman so much that he made him an honorary member of his aristocratic lineage.

When La Farge returned at last to America, it was with a bulging portfolio of canvases and sketches, and a notebook crammed with detailed impressions. These were eventually combined, as a total record of his journey, in *Reminiscences of the South Seas* (1912). In both Europe and America, people were overwhelmed by the elegance of his work and the nobility of the islanders as he had seen them.

The monument to Pierre Loti, erected in 1934 near the pool where he first met Rarahu. Unfortunately, the pool no longer exists

In 1883, Paul Gauguin (1848–1903) found himself an unemployed stockbroker when the Paris stock exchange crashed. His new situation gave him the impetus to try to make a career of painting, which had previously been a weekend hobby. He flirted with Impressionism and Symbolism, but by 1887 was feeling worn down by penury and cold winters. A short working trip to Martinique set him up again, as well as providing a dry run for the much more serious decision to seek out Loti's Tahitian idyll. In April 1891, he set out to leave 'civilization' behind and rejuvenate himself with 'barbarism'. He arrived at Tahiti two weeks after La Farge had left.

Like La Farge, Gauguin was disenchanted by Papeete, finding that its buildings and natives had lost much traditional identity. He chose to dwell instead in a native hut in the district of Mataiea (now the beautiful location of the Gauguin Museum), eventually sharing this with his thirteen-year-old Tahitian 'wife', Tehamana, the subject of many of his paintings. It was due to her that his first stint on the island of just over a year was the happiest time he spent anywhere. He had been driven by loneliness to scour the island for a partner, and had been introduced to Tehamana by her parents at Faone, on the east coast. (By Polynesian standards, she was a mature young woman.) Her name, which means 'Giver of Strength', aptly describes her role in Gauguin's life, and he loved her as much a man could who was so possessed by the demon of his art.

His year on Tahiti was long enough for him to amass sixty-six paintings and a dozen wooden sculptures to take back to Paris. In these, he conspired to capture the melancholy, indolence and nobility of Polynesia's inhabitants. He painted 'what my eyes, veiled by my heart, had seen', rather than attempting any ethnographic, documentary realism. He explored Polynesian mythology, for instance, but often overlaid this with Christian symbolism.

In his first few months upon the island, as he struggled with the unaccustomed heat and humidity, he was struck by the presiding ambience of tranquillity and immobility. This torpor was captured in such paintings as *On the Beach*, *The Bananas*, *Brooding Woman* and *The Siesta*, and is everywhere present in the lolling, slack postures of the islanders. Yet, even after dark, he noted, the inertia is of a different variety to anywhere else: 'The stillness of night in Tahiti is the strangest thing of all. It exists nowhere but here, without so much as a birdcall to disturb one's rest.'

Unlike the other artists visiting the Pacific, Gauguin seemed less struck by the translucent quality of the light than by the exquisitely brilliant tints of the Polynesian complexion. This is reinterpreted over and over in the paintings, just as his notebooks are obsessed with it. He writes of how 'the gold of Tehamana's face flooded all about it' and of the 'orgy of chrome yellows' when the sun touched her. He would stare at her, entranced, for hours.

When he returned to Paris with this new portfolio, it was to an astonished and somewhat antagonistic public and artistic community. They were perplexed by the Polynesian titles, and the artist's personal vision did not correspond with what they understood about the utopia of Tahiti. As Rupert Brooke wrote later: 'Gauguin grossly maligned the ladies. Oh, I know all about expressing their primitive souls by making their bodies square and flat. But it's blasphemy. They're goddesses. He'd have done a Venus De Milo thus.'

A rare picture of Gauguin's fourteen-year-old Tahitian 'wife', Tehamana

Gauguin was an exile in Europe just as much as in Oceania. He returned briefly to Tahiti, but was rejected by Tehamana, who rightly had felt deserted, and eventually left for the island of Hiva Oa in the Marquesas. In the remaining eighteen months of his life, he painted, drew and sculpted prolifically, even though he was terribly ill. He died on the island from a morphine overdose, to escape the agonies of syphilis.

Controversy still reigns today regarding Gauguin's depiction of Tahitian women. Is it simply an element of style which made him render them broad and stocky, or is it really as he saw them? The truth is that as a type he found the Polynesian woman quite beautiful in her own way, but considered her physique caused 'one to mistake her for a man'. She is, 'a Diana the huntress with broad shoulders and narrow hips'. Brooke was not alone in believing that Gauguin was not seeing straight. Yet the artist's compelling, sombre, sometimes disturbingly mystical vision of the islanders has become internationally familiar and accepted as a quite valid response. It must be placed alongside other responses, as filling out the picture, and is often seen as a welcome counterbalance to depictions of Polynesian society that are in an altogether more classical, romantic style.

Henri Matisse (1869–1954) started to paint in 1890, the year that John La Farge left for the South Seas. Matisse abandoned a career as a lawyer's clerk in Paris to become, eventually, one of the most important and influential artists of the century. One of the qualities his work is noted for is an abstract use of pure colour. From 1917, he spent much of his time on the Riviera, where he produced a series of strongly sensual works — tropical fruits and flowers, glowing interiors — vibrant with the sun and rich colours of southern France. The quality of the light was one of the alluring features which would bring him to Oceania. Another was the wish to tread in the footsteps of Gauguin, whose Polynesian work he so admired.

The various stages in the development of Matisse's art were brought about by travel. He had, for example, been to Corsica, Toulouse, even Morocco, but he considered these mere 'changes of scenery' beside the fully-fledged 'voyage' to Tahiti via the United States in 1930. 'I will go to the Islands,' he wrote,

In 1917, W. Somerset Maugham came across this house at Mataiea, Tahiti, where paintings by Gauguin still existed on the glass panels of one of the doors. The artist had decorated the door as a favour to his landlord, who had helped him when he was ill

'to contemplate night and the light of dawn, which probably have a different density in the Tropics.' He sailed from the United States on board the *Tahiti* in March, and was immediately dazzled by colour: 'The sea blue, so blue that it made the sky seem pale … It was a blue like that of the Morpho butterfly …' On arriving at Papeete, he was enraptured: 'I find everything marvellous — landscapes, trees, flowers and people.' He decided that while the light in Europe was 'silver', the light of Oceania was 'all gold'.

Lamentably, despite this initial enthusiasm, Matisse found that he was adversely affected by the heat and humidity to an extent not experienced by previous visiting artists. The enervating effects of this 'steambath' rendered him depressed and incapable of thought and action. He achieved no painting and very little sketching. Amongst the few pen and ink drawings, there is the fishing scene *In Tahiti*, a view from his hotel window in Papeete, another of a clump of coconut trees, and his only life study, *Tahitian Woman* — a sketch of a hotel maid, which she herself disliked. Along with his energy, his enthusiasm ebbed. The pure light of Tahiti was 'beautiful, too beautiful, ferociously beautiful'. He did, however, spend some time alone on a tiny coral atoll some way from the Tahitian mainland, and the experience of taking a glass-bottomed boat across the inner lagoon ('water green as absinthe, very transparent') would stay with him. Lagoons were one of the 'seven wonders of the paradise of painters', and he returned to the subject in later life with a series of 'cut-outs', coloured paper shapes arranged in abstract designs.

The experience of Tahiti had more of a retrospective than an immediate effect upon the art of Matisse. Aspects of the Polynesian experience recur, for instance, in the multiplicity of marine subjects throughout his later work in various media. Oceania even manifested itself in the décor of his apartments in Paris and Nice, through a tropical luxuriance of indoor plants, birds, aquariums and shells. Which is to say that in the case of Matisse the South Seas is, on the whole, only evoked indirectly in his work. He was too shocked by the ferocity of the light, too drained by the sultry climate, to capture properly the full splendour of the islands. One cannot help wishing it had been otherwise. Yet, while Matisse may not have directly evoked many images of Oceania, his own memory of the four-month sojourn was transformed in his work into a dreamy, blissful, colourful ambience, with a prolific use of intense blues. Towards the end of his life, the colours he would use in his cut-outs were so vibrant that his doctor advised him to wear dark glasses — recalling, perhaps, the 'ferociously beautiful' light of the South Seas.

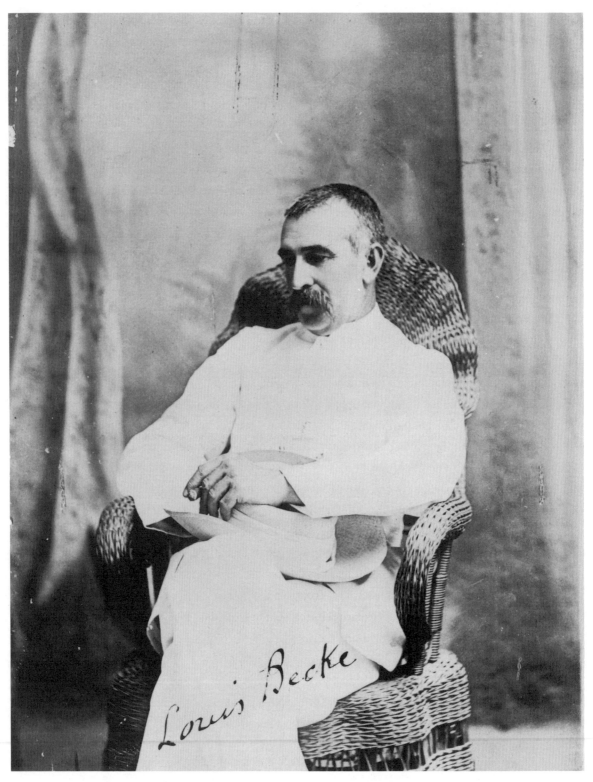

One of the least known but most celebrated cult figures of the South Seas, Louis Becke actually lived
the adventures that he later wrote about

CHAPTER FOUR

THE PEN
AND THE PALM

Visiting Writers of the Nineteenth Century

WRITERS IN SEARCH of a subject have frequently been drawn to uncharted territory and the isolation of the island. Here, in this remote, disconnected and scaled-down world, they are free to create a wide variety of allegory, adventure, romance and social comment. Even prior to the discoveries of the great explorers of the South Seas, rumours and sightings of distant tropical islands had inspired books. Daniel Defoe's *Robinson Crusoe* (1719) was based on the true account of Alexander Selkirk's survival on an island off the Pacific coast of South America. In 1726, Swift published *Gulliver's Travels*, with maps showing islands which lay within uncharted regions of the Pacific.

After the appearance of the published accounts of the circumnavigators, this literature had more substance and romance on which to feed. Coleridge's *The Rime of the Ancient Mariner* (1798), for instance, is indebted to Cook's voyages. Byron, too, whose grandfather had sailed in the *Dolphin* to the South Seas, based his narrative poem *The Island* (1823) mainly upon Bligh's chronicle of the mutiny on the *Bounty*, and partly on William Mariner's *Account of the Tonga Islands* (1817). In the second stanza, Byron rapturously describes the sailors as, 'Young hearts, which languish'd for some sunny isle / Where summer years and summer women smile.'

Armchair-bound tropical island writers would, of course, continue to ply their popular trade, even after the great Melville's real-life experience had put them in the shade. It still gave more leeway to the imagination, and enabled them lazily to mine a rich and lucrative vein. Children's authors, for instance, played fast and loose with the South Pacific isle in Wyss's entertainingly ridiculous *Swiss Family Robinson* (1813) and Ballantyne's *Coral Island* (1858). In the former, for instance, there are monster snakes on the island, and in the latter penguins. Both continue to cast their dubious spell over the young at heart, whereas the often excellent, now unfashionable, Captain Marryat created a much more sober, gripping adolescent drama of Pacific desert island survival in *Masterman Ready* (1841). Marryat's novel could almost be used as a self-survival manual for the coral island castaway.

True South Pacific literature began with American author Herman Melville (1819–91). Just as Sydney Parkinson was the first important artist actually to visit and paint the islands, Melville was the first to write about them from up close. His trailblazing voyage there in 1841, at the tender age of twenty-two, set the trend for all subsequent writer–adventurers in Oceania. It was practically compulsory for everyone who came afterwards to visit his first port of call — the Taipi-Vai Valley on Nuku Hiva in the Marquesas — as if it were some kind of literary Mecca. Stevenson came to the South Pacific almost entirely due to Melville's example, then found himself in turn an object of

Taken after 1850, this shot of Papeete shows a verdant town, with the Queen's palace in the foreground and the royal retreat of Motu Utu out in the lagoon. The contemporary colour shot (see page 79), from a similar angle, reveals how the docks have spread out to encompass this little island

reverence. Indeed, Oceania became the destination of an alternative Grand Tour for a whole string of writers, right up to contemporary travel writer and novelist Paul Theroux.

None of those who followed had anywhere near the romantic adventures which awaited the young Melville in the South Seas. Just as his whaling ship, the *Acushnet*, hove to in Nuku Hiva's spectacular Taiohae Bay, there clambered aboard 'a shoal of whihenies [vahines] … their jet-black tresses streaming over their shoulders, and half enveloping their otherwise naked forms'. Such a voluptuous introduction to the islands led to Melville and fellow malcontent Richard T. Green ('Toby' in the book) both jumping ship at the first opportunity. Life on board a nineteenth-century whaler was, after all, hardly the *QEII*, and the green valleys called, with their smoking waterfalls and towering peaks.

What happened to Melville in the near-fabulous Taipi-Vai Valley (related in his novel *Typee*) was to become a golden legend of the modern Pacific — one to set alongside Loti's extraordinary experience in Tahiti's Fautaua Valley. This Edenic Marquesan location, filled with fruit trees and graced with a small lake, was home to the supposedly cannibal tribe the Taipis, in whose company the pair of young men were not altogether at ease. But nothing terrible befell them, and for Melville the central attraction of the valley proved to be 'the beauteous nymph Fayaway, who was my peculiar favorite'. Dressed predominantly in her mane of rich brown hair, which 'hid from view her lovely bosom', it was lust, if not love, at first sight. And, just as Loti's experience of the South Seas is magically condensed into a single incident beside the Fautaua Falls, Melville concentrates the romantic and exotic allure of Oceania into one resonant moment.

One hot, lethargic day, he is disporting upon the cool lake with Fayaway and her delightful female companions, engaged in the agreeable contact sport of swimming after and pulling under the young ladies. Suddenly, Fayaway dreams up a new game in the small boat:

> *With a wild exclamation of delight, she disengaged from her person the ample robe of tappa … and spreading it out like a sail, stood erect with upraised arms in the head of the canoe. We American sailors pride ourselves upon our straight clean spars, but a prettier little mast than Fayaway made was never shipped aboard any craft.*

It was an incident so charged with erotic South Sea colour that the American artist John La Farge felt moved to sketch it. Whether truth or fiction, Melville here creates a character as vivid as Loti's little Rarahu or Webber's Poedua.

Melville later visited Tahiti and its sister island of Moorea, and from these experiences composed his second novel, *Omoo*. The chronicle of a contented, time-wasting beachcomber, *Omoo* is more relaxed, lighter in tone than *Typee*. It was *Typee*, however, which caught the imagination of the public. Published simultaneously in Great Britain and the United States, it was to be Melville's most popular work well into the twentieth century (and that includes *Moby-Dick*). His thrilling accounts of his adventures were also popular in the form of a lucrative series of talks, which he gave up and down the country shortly after his return from the Pacific. The forcefulness of his personal narrations even stirred some intrepid souls to follow in his footsteps. Among these was Herman's brother, Tom, who joined a whaling cruise in March 1846.

Beside the more conventional travel writing of *Omoo*, *Typee* plugs into the darkly mysterious, languid and sensual ambience of the South Seas. And, since we know exaggeration is involved, we can assume that, to some extent, his book contributed to this ambience, much like the early painting. The truth is that he was, for instance, only in the valley for a very short time, and was always closer to safety than he suggests. Nevertheless, his readers were ravished by the spell of Melville's Oceania, even though American religious magazines could not approve of his anti-missionary stance or Fayaway's brazen impudence.

The next literary visitor to the isles was a distinct contrast to Melville. Compared with the latter's intrepid arrival aboard a whaling ship, and the robust nature of his novels, American poet Charles Warren Stoddard (1843–1909) was a gentle aesthete. Although very popular and influential at the time, Stoddard's books about his Oceanic travels have gone out of fashion. They were once, however, admired by the likes of Mark Twain and Robert Louis Stevenson, being instrumental in their own choice to visit the region. The major book which arose from Stoddard's experiences, *South-Sea Idyls* (reprinted in London as *Summer Cruising in the South Seas*, 1874), is a warm and charming collection of impressions.

Stoddard was a kind and sweet-tempered man with a whimsical sense of humour — particularly after a few drinks. His doctor had told him to travel to improve his generally bad health, and he had chosen the islands after reading Melville. However, he was not so delicate that 'roughing it' was out of the question. In order to glimpse the realities of island life, and to strike up relationships with the islanders, he would frequently sleep outdoors, or accept an invitation to be the guest of a native family.

Between 1864 and 1873, Stoddard undertook three trips to Hawaii and one to Tahiti. As mentioned elsewhere (see Introduction), Stoddard was gay, unattached and very romantic by nature. In the company of close friends, he was open about his sexual proclivities, but had the sense in his literature to only leave clues (sometimes quite obvious) for those in the know. As far as one can glean, he enjoyed the company of six handsome Hawaiian youths and one Tahitian.

One young man in particular seems to have captured Stoddard's affections, in an episode which matches the amorous interludes of Melville and Loti. In 1868, in the Halawa Valley, on eastern Molokai, he meets Kana-ana, with whom he whiles away several days, maybe weeks — he loses track. 'We two lay upon an enormous old-fashioned bed with high posts … He would mesmerize me into a most refreshing sleep with a prolonged and pleasing manipulation.' What Stoddard's average reader, or even his publisher, made of all this, one cannot imagine.

Down and out in Tahiti in 1870, he delightedly fell in with the indolence of island life. Papeete was in the midst of its mid-August Fête Napoleon, with waltzing in the grounds of the Governor's house, and Polynesian dancing in the gardens of Queen Pomare's palace. It was, however, the islanders and their subtle skin colour that drove him to wax lyrical:

They were olive tinted and this tint was of the tenderest olive; of the olive that has a shade of gold in it like a honey-comb that has entangled a sunbeam and is therewith transfigured; and some were of a softer shade, as if the film of a shadow had fallen upon them and would not go away — for these were children of the sun and he had set his seal upon them forever.

Stoddard spent perhaps the best years of his life upon the islands, and certainly wrote his best books about them. In the final months before his death, bedridden with a weak heart at his home in Monteray, his head was filled with innumerable exotic and romantic memories. It is said that he preferred these even to the company of his friends.

Although it was Stoddard's enthusiasm which interested Mark Twain in visiting Hawaii, he actually went there on the purely practical basis of a journalistic commission. His real name was Samuel Langhorne Clemens (1835–1910), and he was first published under the pseudonym Mark Twain for a volume of collected letters, written from the Sandwich Islands (Hawaii), for original publication in the *Sacramento Union*. These extremely popular letters, twenty-five in all, appeared in the paper on a weekly basis, for which Clemens was paid $20 a piece. They were his first sustained writing — an enormously entertaining blend of travelogue, anecdote and news reporting. He used them not only as a means to develop his incisive wit, but to convey to the reader the exotic splendours of island life. It would be no exaggeration to say that he went there to do a job, but fell head over heels for Hawaii, and several times even contemplated making the islands his home.

Twain departed for Honolulu in March 1866, on the steamer *Ajax*. The future fiftieth state of the USA was then the realm of His Majesty Kamehameha V, and its capital bore little resemblance to the high-rise modern American city of today. Twain found lodgings in a small cottage with a huge tamarind tree in the garden, and hired a rather lazy, disobedient horse as transport around Oahu. He loved his food and drink, and although the missionaries had had a sobering effect on the islanders, Twain enjoyed his daily whisky all the more for their disapproval. Trying out a few new foods, he could not approve of the bitter tamarind fruit: 'They sharpened my teeth up like a razor, and put a wire edge on them that I think likely will wear off when the enamel does.' As for poi, a native dish of breadfruit porridge, 'it produces acrid humors, a fact which sufficiently accounts for the blithe and humorous character of the Kanakas'.

On his travels, he came across 'a large company of naked natives, of both sexes and all ages, amusing themselves with the national pastime of surf-bathing'. His account of surfing seems to be the first written report of the sport, just as Webber painted probably the first visual record. On a side trip to the Big Island, Twain was intrigued to visit Kealakekua Bay, where Captain Cook was killed, and delighted in reporting the rumour that the great man's heart, removed from his body, was eaten by three children who mistook it for dog. Later, standing beside the active crater of Kilauea, he wrote that, 'The smell of sulphur is strong, but not unpleasant to a sinner.' At Waiohinu, on the south of the Big Island, he planted a monkeypod tree, which grew to a considerable height, and stood for almost a century, until it was felled by a storm in 1957.

Twain returned from the islands in July short of cash. To try to earn a little extra, he decided to lecture on his experiences at the San Francisco Academy of Music. The talk was rather dryly entitled 'Our Fellow Savages of the Sandwich Islands', and was very enthusiastically received. This experience so encouraged Twain that he went on to become one of the most popular public speakers of his time, with the subject of the islands as his favourite topic. His wry but kindly attitude towards Hawaii and its natives provided a friendly and colourful image that attracted his audiences to a group of islands which ceded itself to the USA in 1898 and was admitted to the Union in 1959.

Over seventy years before James A. Michener dreamed up Bali-h'ai, Louis Marie Julien Viaud (1850–1923), adopting the name Pierre Loti, created for his readers a seductive, moody picture of paradise in his semi-autobiographical novel *The Marriage of Loti*. His book describes a young seaman's interlude on Tahiti, from 1872–73, particularly his romance with the lovely vahine Rarahu, a Polynesian girl attached to the court of Queen Pomare. It was Loti, as much as Melville, who popularized the languid, sensuous side of the South Seas, and it was his book which fired Paul Gauguin to flee to Polynesia.

Loti was something of a Gallic-style Byron, though somewhat less physically imposing. Here was another poetic soul, much given to dressing up in the exotic costumes of other cultures, greatly attracted to travel and romantic intrigue. On board the flagship *Flore*, Midshipman Viaud sailed to Tahiti via Easter Island and the Marquesas, sketching and noting his impressions along the way. When eventually he stepped ashore at Tahiti, his first reaction was how bowed the islanders seemed by the iron rule of the missionaries. The spell of the island soon overcame this, however. Loti settled down to enjoy the tail-end of the reign of the celebrated Tahitian regent Queen Pomare IV, under whose rule traditional island lifestyles were in the main still preserved. Pierre quickly 'went native', dressing in a pareu, sleeping upon a straw mat, eating guavas and breadfruit, learning the customs and language. Given generous shore leave by his admiral, he quickly slipped into the native way of 'utter idleness and perpetual dreaming'.

One day, Loti headed north out of Tahiti, on the road to Apire (now Pirae), where he turned right and entered a shady valley, discovering a place where rock pools were fed by the Fautaua Falls. In one of these, he contentedly watched a group of young Tahitian women bathing: 'Large black butterflies fluttered languidly past, or rested on us, as though their sheeny wings were too heavy to bear them; the air was charged with heady and unfamiliar perfume …' It is as if Loti is drugged, or in a dream; everything moves slowly, and details are exaggerated. Soon, our lotus-eater hero is lost in the silken embrace of the fifteen-year-old Rarahu, and a new South Sea myth is born.

The couple were encouraged by the Queen to marry, Tahitian-style. In a state of romantic somnambulance, the two young people wandered the glades and palace grounds together for two months, until it was time for Loti's ship to depart. By this time, our hero was beginning to worry that without the ship to wrest him from the island, he might have been trapped there under an everlasting spell.

The town of Papeete, Tahiti, as it is today. Compared to the archive photograph, taken in the second half of the nineteenth century, (see page 74) *the buildings and docks have spread considerably*

Taiohae Bay, on the island of Nuku Hiva, in the Marquesas, where Melville's ship, the Acushnet, *hove to in 1841.*
Its spectacular beauty encouraged him to jump ship

Apia, the capital of Western Samoa, on the island of Upolu. With white frame houses and churches spreading around the bay,
it looks today very much as it did when Stevenson first saw it

Stevenson's home on the slopes above Apia, on the island of Upolu, Western Samoa.
Today it is part museum, part Government House

The pool in which Loti spied Rarahu bathing.
Situated in the Fautaua Valley, outside Papeete, Tahiti,
this photo was taken early this century, before it was cemented
over as part of the town's water supply

The pace of Loti's life had slowed down to a delicious inertia: 'Those who have lived in the tropics know the enervating luxury of that noon-day slumber … dreaming or sleeping to the soothing chirp of the grasshoppers.' Even when awake, he was trapped in a delightful routine of pleasurable occupations: playing cards with Rarahu and her companions, drifting about the lagoon in a canoe, diving for shells and coral and gazing at the Southern Cross in the night sky.

The Marriage of Loti is essentially what really happened to the young seaman, even if there are poetic emphases and transformations for the sake of the story. Some have called the book sentimental, but others would hold that it is not. Loti's novel is, instead, romantic in the true sense of the term, capturing the feelings of an impressionable, pleasure-loving young man in a strange land richly endowed by nature. The public reaction to the book back home was wholehearted approval. The French nation was then relatively static and its people untravelled, and Loti's novel took them on a magic carpet ride not to be forgotten.

Marcel Proust, Anatole France and Alexandre Dumas were among the fellow writers who admired the book, and it was reprinted several times in Paris, London and New York. Shops sold Rarahu ribbons, like the one the hero gave his heroine, and Loti bon-bons were exchanged as lovers' presents. By 1898, Reynaldo Hahn had turned the book into an operetta, *L'Ille du rêve*, which opened at the Paris Opéra Comique. (Six years later, Puccini would base his more famous opera, *Madame Butterfly*, upon Loti's novel *Madame Chrysanthème*.)

Loti attended the opening night of *L'Ille du rêve*. As the curtain rose on Act One, set at the falls, he was so moved by his memories that he was forced to leave the theatre, and walked the streets of Paris in tears. When he returned, for the final act, he was in time to catch a bereft Rarahu cry out to him: 'Loti! Loti!' It was more than he could bear. The South Seas' 'rêve' into which his book had plunged a nation, was bitter–sweet to the author, who recalled again the face of the real Rarahu, his first love.

The most celebrated of the region's literary figures is Robert Louis Stevenson (1850–94), although the importance of Oceania to his life and work is seldom sufficiently acknowledged. Stevenson spent the last six years of his life in the South Seas. Its climate stabilized his frail health, and its people and beauty provided material and inspiration for stories — many of them actually set elsewhere. His invaluable contribution to Pacific literature includes the brilliant travel account *In the South Seas* (1890), one of his best short stories, 'The Beach of Falesa' (1893), and *The Ebb-Tide* (1894), a stirring adventure novel co-written with his stepson, Lloyd Osbourne.

Stevenson needed Oceania as much as it needed him. Shortly after his marriage in 1880 to the American divorcee Fanny Osbourne, he began a struggle with tuberculosis, which would have claimed him

The face of Rarahu, as sketched by a smitten Loti. 'Her eyes were of a tawny black, full of exotic languor and coaxing softness'

sooner were it not for the congenial weather of the South Seas. In 1888, the whole family, including Louis' mother, left on the hired schooner *Casco* to seek out the life-giving, balmy climate of the Pacific. The boat's captain, A.H. Otis, had taken one look at the stick-like frame of his passenger and immediately included among the *Casco*'s trappings all that was necessary for a funeral at sea. Louis felt fine, however. 'I am never well but at sea,' he boasted. At under 5 foot 9 (175 centimetres), and weighing less than a 150 pounds (68 kilos), he stripped down to singlet and trousers and went barefoot: 'As for colour, hands, arms, feet, legs, and face, I am browner than the berry; only my trunk and the aristocratic spot on which I sit retain the vile whiteness of the north.'

At the Marquesas, they paid their respects to Melville, sailed down through the Tuamotu atolls, and on to Tahiti. Despite his boasts, Louis was very ill here, and they waited for him to recover at Tautira, an idyllic, half-wild spot on the island's southern peninsula. They were so happy here that, when she returned to London, Stevenson's mother sent the local Protestant church a silver communion set, which is still being used today.

The family searched the South Pacific very thoroughly until, at last, they came across Apia, on the north coast of Upolu, in Samoa. The climate here was perfect for Louis, especially the slopes behind the town, which benefited from the fresh sea breezes, and the mail service was one of the best in the Pacific. What is more, Louis immediately became entangled in the political struggles of the islanders against the three competing powers of Germany, Britain and the United States, who were vying for dominion over Samoa. In this way, Stevenson did not merely live in Samoa, he interacted with it on behalf of his Samoan brethren. In various pieces of writing, he represented them to the world, and he frequently used his name to expedite political matters.

The Stevensons paid $4,000 for 400 acres (162 hectares) of land:

We range from 600 to 1,500 feet, have five streams, waterfalls, precipices, profound ravines, rich tablelands, 50 head of cattle on the ground (if anyone could catch them), a great view of forest, sea and mountains, the war-ships in the haven: really a noble place.

Here they built the huge two-storeyed wooden frame house known as Vailima — recently restored as part Government House of Western Samoa, and part Stevenson Museum. On an enclosed first-floor veranda, Louis did his writing, and in the great hall, lined with Californian redwood, he entertained islanders and visiting friends as if he were laird. Even his native staff were attired in loin-cloths of the royal Stuart tartan.

Among their many visitors was the historian Henry Adams. The reliability of his evidence is difficult to gauge, but he gave the impression in a letter that the set-up at Vailima was rather less than

Family and servants on the steps of the house at Vailima; left to right: Joe Strong, Auvea (a plantation hand), Mary Carter (maid to Mrs M.I. Stevenson), Mrs M.I. Stevenson, Elena, Lloyd Osbourne, Arrick, Talolo, RLS, Austin Strong, Fanny Stevenson, Isobel Strong, Simi (butler), Lafaele and Tomasi

picturesque. He described the house as 'a two-storey Irish shanty' with 'squalor like a railroad navvy's board hut'. Furthermore, Louis was in 'dirty striped pyjamas' and was like 'a bundle of sticks in a bag', while Fanny was labelled 'a wild Apache'. Perhaps the Stevensons were taken by surprise, and unprepared for their guest. As it was, feelings were very much mutual, as Louis did not care for Adams's toffee-nosed sarcasm, and was only too happy to bid him farewell.

In order to support himself and his family at Vailima, for the last six years of his life Stevenson was more prolific with his pen than at any other time. He finished a dozen books and started several more. Although *In the South Seas* was not a great commercial success, his other work from this period did well, and was usually serialised in such magazines as the *Illustrated London News*. While *The Ebb-Tide* and 'The Beach of Falesa' presented an image of the harshness of Pacific life, and one which Victorian readers back home found rather strong meat, his delightful short stories 'The Isle of Voices' and 'The Bottle Imp' revealed the more gentle, exotic, whimsical side of island life.

Unusually, 'The Bottle Imp' appeared in the Samoan language almost simultaneously with its publication in English, having been translated by a local missionary. Which only goes to show that Stevenson's magic, his gift as Tusitala ('Teller of Tales'), was as potent to his Samoan brethren as to his English-speaking readership. His fame, as representative of the gentleman artist abroad, fed back into the South Pacific so that today you may stay at Apia's Tusitala Hotel and order a glass of Vailima beer. This is not, however, just rank commercialism. More than any other visiting Westerner, Stevenson found his way to the heart of the Polynesian people.

In December 1894, Louis died of a cerebral haemorrhage — while preparing the dressing for a salad. It was as sudden as it was merciful. He was buried on the summit of Mount Vaea, behind Vailima. Many of the tearful Samoan friends who carried his body up there, cutting a trail through the bush which can still be followed, were the same people who had, as a gift, built 'The Road of Loving Hearts' up to his house. The tomb, which also contains the body of Fanny, overlooks the mountains, the home, the town, the reef and the ocean which had come to mean so much to him.

It has become an unspoken rule that all Oceanic literary visitors should climb Mount Vaea and pay their respects at this monument, which has become for them something of a Mecca of the South Seas. And all those who reach the summit, wiping away the perspiration of the ascent, see on the side of his tomb, Louis' famous, moving requiem:

> *This be the verse you grave for me:*
> *Here he lies where he longed to be;*
> *Home is the sailor, home from the sea,*
> *And the hunter home from the hill.*

One of the most compelling South Sea authors is also the least known. Louis Becke (1855–1913), one of the best of Australia's short story writers, made the Pacific his adventure playground. Ranging from Papua New Guinea to Easter Island, his tales live and breathe the air of Oceania, with the kind of relaxed and intimate feel that only comes from total familiarity with the subject. Becke never views the South Pacific through rosy spectacles: he wrote about exactly what he saw. His collections *By Reef and Palm* (1894), *The Ebbing of the Tide* (1896) and *Pacific Tales* (1897), combine Jack London's feel for rollicking adventure with Somerset Maugham's jaundiced eye for human vulnerability.

From early childhood, Becke was never able to settle. He ran away from his New South Wales home twice before he was ten, and by fourteen he was on a ship heading for San Francisco. Once he had tasted the peculiar flavour of the Pacific, there was no going back for him. Though several times he attempted to make a home for himself back in Australia, only bad health finally kept him from his beloved islands. His first job in the Pacific was at Apia, in Samoa, where he worked as a store clerk. His experience here led to several remote and lonely postings as a trader, first on the Ellice islands of Nanumanga and Nukufetau, where he was plagued by hurricanes, then on New Britain (an island in the Bismarck Archipelago), where he lived in terror of cannibal attacks and contracted malaria. Nothing, however, could put Louis off roaming the islands, searching for adventure while there was still breath left in him. The only thing he feared was dying in bed with his boots off.

When he was only eighteen, he had accepted the challenge of a job as a ship's 'supercargo' — an administrative position controlling a voyage's commercial affairs. Ships then, as now, supplied goods to remote island traders in return for local products such as copra and pearl shell. It was through this job that Becke came to work for the infamous, piratical South Sea figure of Bully Hayes. The American-born Hayes had raped and plundered his way across the Pacific for some twenty years, his most iniquitous practice being blackbirding, or slave-trading. The young Louis worked as supercargo for Hayes for a short period, but even Becke's taste for danger and action could not keep him for long with such a scoundrel.

By 1892, marriage and a recurrence of his malaria found Louis back in Australia. To pass the time, he would spin yarns about the life he had led, or from rumours he had heard while travelling among the islands. Explorer and author Ernest Favenc himself was intrigued by the tales and recommended Becke to approach the editor of the *Bulletin* magazine. As a trial piece, Becke wrote up one of his exploits in the same spare, immediate style in which he used to tell them. Six more stories followed, all written in long-hand on a table of old gin cases pushed together. These eventually formed the basis of the collection *By Reef and Palm*, for which Louis was hailed 'the Rudyard Kipling of the Pacific'.

Becke became a prolific writer, even though he made little money from his skill, preferring to sell his books outright and not to bother with royalties. He was fêted in European literary circles and even lived in London for a while. People were fascinated both by his dark, exotic tales and by the man himself. One English journalist interviewed him in a London pub and was startled at the way he shouted for his drinks and by his huge, powerful hands: 'They look strong enough to crush a coconut, or a skull.' None the less, Becke was at this stage too ill to return to the islands. He died of throat cancer at seventy-eight, and was found slumped in a chair, with the manuscript of an unfinished story spread out over the table before him. His boots were on.

One of only two photographs which exist of Rupert Brooke's Tahitian lover, Taatamata, daughter of a village chief

CHAPTER FIVE

CRUSOE AND THE KEYBOARD

Literary Ramblers of the Twentieth Century

FROM JACK LONDON at the beginning of the century to Paul Theroux close to its conclusion, roving writers have continued to head for the South Seas. Daring it to deliver all its promised enchantment — the ultimate test case for the credibility of heaven on earth — they have poked about in all its corners, comparing what they saw with previous accounts. By the time Theroux entered the arena in the early 1990s, a developing, post-war Pacific seemed more disorientating than comforting. Yet he, too, eventually discovered a kind of paradise, and certainly came upon as much adventure as any visitor to Oceania.

The earliest of the century's literary wanderers, Jack London (1876–1916), once wrote: 'Life that lives is life successful.' As writer and roisterer, he did all he could to live up to his maxim, and certainly gave the adventure-loving Melville a run for his money. While London's name is primarily associated with northern American dramas of survival such as *The Call of the Wild* and *White Fang*, one of his major passions was the South Pacific, and he wrote nearly a dozen volumes about it — travel writing, short stories and novels. His harrowing, sometimes blissful experiences in Oceania are reflected particularly in the three volumes of short stories, *South Sea Tales* (1911), *The House of Pride and Other Tales of Hawaii* (1912) and *On the Makaloa Mat* (1919). The South Seas, though, proved more of a challenge than he had bargained for, becoming his final obsession and his nemesis.

What gave Jack the notion of visiting the Pacific in the first place was the attraction of the pattern set by Melville and Stevenson. More immediately, however, when fellow socialists in America

Jack London at Waikiki, 1907. On either side of him, in the centre of the group,
are his wife Charmian and cook Martin Johnson

began to question his well-heeled lifestyle, not to mention the individualism his novels seemed to preach, London thought it time to put his plans into action. The Pacific would give him time and space to think things through, and perhaps provide an adventure to boot. And so it was that in 1907, accompanied by his second wife, Charmian Kittredge, he left San Francisco in a home-designed 45-foot (14-metre) ketch called the *Snark*. It was a journey which would take him to Hawaii, the Marquesas, Tahiti, Samoa, Fiji, the New Hebrides and the Solomons. This epic voyage, with its combination of grave health problems on board and exotic thrills wherever they anchored, would plunge Jack at one moment into the profoundest gloom he had known, and at another, lift his spirits higher than he would have believed possible.

In the stories and articles London sent back from the Pacific, to be published in such North American magazines as the highly prestigious *Atlantic Monthly*, he portrayed in the main the harsher realities of Oceanic life. In Tahiti, rather than romance, he depicted the sometimes unsympathetic French overlordship in the short story 'The Chinago', the pathetic tale of a little Chinese man up against unyielding authority. Similarly, 'Koolau the Leper' traces the tragedy of a native Hawaiian afflicted by the introduced disease, attempting to hold out against virtual imprisonment in the leper colony of Molokai. With his socialist sympathies, Jack would often feature the lot of the disenfranchised islander, bringing out an inherent heroism in his central characters. Like Stevenson,

London told the world about the obverse side of European development in the South Seas, firmly empathizing with the victims.

Not all London's Oceanic writing took this serious tone, however. *The Cruise of the Snark* (1911), Jack's account of his tremendous voyage, conveys the mysterious otherness and the adventure of the islands, with brisk action and vivid personalities at every turn. At Tahiti, for example, London was intrigued to meet the prototype Californian hippie Ernest Darling, with whom he boxed for fun and conversed for hours about the Nature Man's belief in the benefits of nudism. 'His laundry bill cannot be large!' Jack quipped. Darling was a fruitarian who had established a small commune on the lonely, southernmost tip of the island's peninsula. In 1924, novelist and fisherman Zane Grey also reported coming across Ernest.

Jack's own philosophy of machismo found another instance of manly physicality in the Hawaiians who surfed in the pounding breakers off Waikiki Beach. London's vivid and dramatic description popularized the sport and the place overnight. This was no mere leisure activity, but man challenging the very gods as he struggles with the surf:

> *… his feet buried in the churning foam, the salt smoke rising to his knees, and all the rest of him in the free air and flashing sun-light, and he is flying through the air, flying forward, flying fast as the surge on which he stands. He is Mercury — a brown Mercury.*

Jack thus laid down a whole metaphysics of surfing, variations of which underly the tenets of its serious adherents to this day. Such beliefs can be seen to good effect in Hollywood's philosophical surfing epic *Big Wednesday* (1978).

When Jack tried to surf himself, he was rewarded for his efforts with severe sunburn which laid him low for days. In the final analysis, the trip became London's personal 'heart of darkness' when the body he regarded as that of some superman badly let him down. Partly through poor diet on board, and partly due to his neurotic need to feel dominant, Jack was tormented at different stages of the voyage by malaria, psoriasis, yaws (ulcers caused by bacterial infection), toothache and a rectal fistula (an abnormal passage, caused by an abscess, between the bowel and the body surface). It did not help that his wife's health remained annoyingly stable throughout the voyage.

In November 1908, he was forced to call off the trip. He returned to his ranch outside San Francisco, but his health had been dealt a severe blow by the trying conditions of the South Pacific. In 1916, he was found dead with two empty phials of morphine beside his bed. His greatest adventure, which he had shared with millions of readers, had been an adventure too far. He had, in effect, tested himself against the surfing gods of Hawaii and achieved only his own 'wipeout'.

An exceptionally handsome young man who died at the tender age of twenty-eight, Rupert Brooke (1887–1915) has become something of a cultish literary hero. Dying young while still at the height of their powers has always added glamour to the myths of such idolized public figures as James Dean and Montgomery Clift. The most improbably romantic thing about the life of Rupert Brooke,

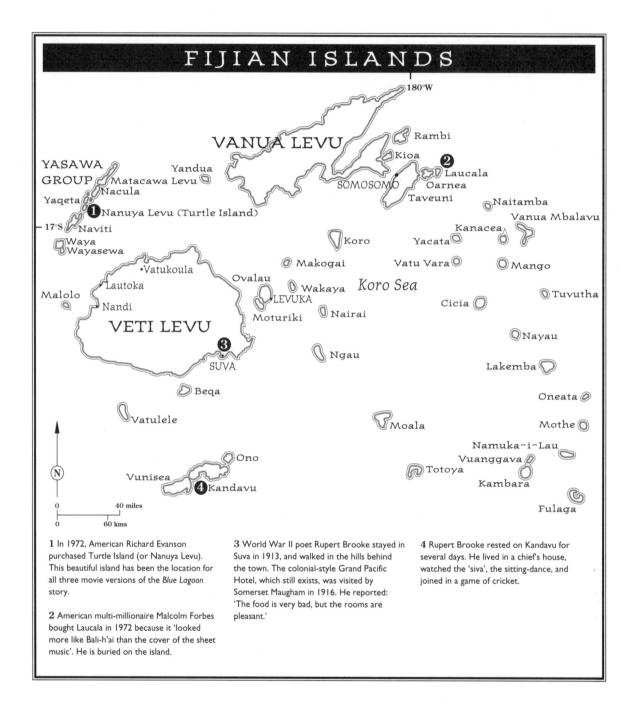

FIJIAN ISLANDS

180°W

VANUA LEVU

Rambi

Kioa

Laucala ❷

Oarnea

SOMOSOMO

Taveuni

Naitamba

YASAWA
GROUP

Yandua

Matacawa Levu

Nacula

Vanua Mbalavu

Yaqeta

Kanacea

Nanuya Levu (Turtle Island) ❶

17°S   Naviti

Koro

Yacata

Mango

Waya
Wayasewa

Makogai

Vatu Vara

Vatukoula

Ovalau

Koro Sea

Malolo

Lautoka

Wakaya

Tuvutha

LEVUKA

Nandi

Moturiki

Nairai

Cicia

VETI LEVU

Nayau

❸

Ngau

Lakemba

SUVA

Beqa

Oneata

Vatulele

Moala

Mothe

Namuka-i-Lau

N

Ono

Vuanggava

Vunisea

Totoya

❹ Kandavu

Kambara

0   40 miles

0   60 kms

Fulaga

1 In 1972, American Richard Evanson purchased Turtle Island (or Nanuya Levu). This beautiful island has been the location for all three movie versions of the *Blue Lagoon* story.

2 American multi-millionaire Malcolm Forbes bought Laucala in 1972 because it 'looked more like Bali-h'ai than the cover of the sheet music'. He is buried on the island.

3 World War II poet Rupert Brooke stayed in Suva in 1913, and walked in the hills behind the town. The colonial-style Grand Pacific Hotel, which still exists, was visited by Somerset Maugham in 1916. He reported: 'The food is very bad, but the rooms are pleasant.'

4 Rupert Brooke rested on Kandavu for several days. He lived in a chief's house, watched the 'siva', the sitting-dance, and joined in a game of cricket.

though, is his little-known dalliance with a Tahitian woman in whose arms he recovered from the hurt inflicted by the love of his life, Katherine Cox.

The fact that Brooke even visited the South Seas comes as a surprise to most people, who recall him only as composing some of the most popular poetry of World War I, and being buried in the idyllic splendour of an olive grove on a Greek island. He visited Oceania on the recommendation of his friends, who saw him with a broken heart and on the verge of a nervous breakdown. He had fallen madly in love with fellow student Katherine Cox at Cambridge University, and felt lost and humiliated when she was incapable of returning his affections. His friends thus suggested a trip around the world, which would be financed by articles based on his impressions, posting them as he travelled to such publications as the *Westminster Gazette* and the *New Statesman*. He finally departed in May 1913 for New York, and by October had decided to extend his expedition, setting sail on the SS *Sierra* for Hawaii.

Travelling amongst the islands — Hawaii, Samoa, Fiji — Rupert, in his way, made endless friends, found that the stars seemed nearer at night, and was beginning to feel this was 'like living in a Keats world, only less syrupy'. 'In the South Seas the Creator seems to have laid himself out to show what He can do,' he reported in the *New Statesman*. Upon reaching Tahiti in January 1914, he was actually not over-keen on the hot and stuffy capital of Papeete, but thought he would try the southern village of Mataiea, where Gauguin had lived. Here he found 'the most ideal place in the world to live in and work in'. He obtained a room and meals at a large, rambling colonial-style house with a wooden pier at the bottom of the garden, which jutted out into the luminous green waters of the lagoon. He slopped around barefoot all day in an old vest and native pareu, diving off the pier to

Rupert Brooke (second from right) *and friends outside his lodgings in the village of Mataiea, Tahiti*

cool down whenever the fancy took him. However, he began to discover that, although the bright and warm ambience sensitized him to water, light and air, 'If you live the South Sea life, the intellect soon lapses into quiescence.'

None the less, it was here that Rupert wrote 'Tiare Tahiti', the heroine of which is Taatamata, daughter of the village chief. She called him Pupure ('Fair'), he called her by her pet name of Mamua, and they were seldom apart. He was a strong swimmer and they swam together every day, even under the bright light of the Polynesian moon. Mamua had her rivals, however. At a local wedding, Rupert endeared himself to the assembly by dancing the upa-upa, and ended up being proposed to by the new bride.

Of Mamua herself, little is actually known. There are two photographs and, of course, what Brooke recorded in letters and notes. Their idyll drew to a close when he cut his leg one day on coral, and was forced to seek medical aid in Papeete. Mamua went with him. 'I have been nursed and waited on by a girl with wonderful eyes, the walk of a goddess, and the heart of an angel, who is, luckily, devoted to me,' he wrote. 'She gives her time to ministering to me, I mine to probing her queer mind. I think I shall write a book about her — only I fear I'm too fond of her.'

Arthur Grimble in the Residency on Ocean Island (or Banaba)

He tore himself away from Tahiti in April, 'not without tears'. Even the charms of Mamua and the islands could not cut the bonds which tied him to his own culture. But that was not an end to it. A year later, he received a letter from her, addressed to 'My dear love darling'. A month before he died on the Greek island of Scyros, Rupert left an envelope with a friend to be opened in case of emergency. The letter contained the paragraph: 'Try to inform Taata of my death. Mlle Taata, Hotel Tiare, Papeete, Tahiti. It might find her. Give her my love.' She was, thus, on his mind to the last. Perhaps in his final hours, as the fever played tricks with his mind, Rupert was transported once again to Mataiea:

> *… Mamua*
> *Crown the hair, and come away!*
> *Hear the calling of the moon*
> *And the whispering scents that stray*
> *Above the idle warm lagoon.*
>
> 'TIARE TAHITI'

No visiting writer to the South Pacific could be more of a contrast to the others than Sir Arthur Grimble (1888–1956). Unlike the adventurers Melville and London, or romantics such as Loti and Brooke, Grimble was a mild-mannered, smartly-dressed, sensible British gentleman. Always the first to parody his appearance, he once described himself as 'tallish, pinkish, long-nosed … fantastically thin-legged and dolefully mild of manner'. Nevertheless, he wrote full-bloodedly and with great flamboyance about the splendours of Oceania, and his love for the islanders was unbounded. In March 1914, he left England with his wife Olivia to work for the Colonial Service in the Gilbert and Ellice Islands. He would be there, on and off, until 1932, working in a range of posts on a variety of the group's islands.

In *A Pattern of Islands* (1952) and *Return to the Islands* (1957), we have a warm, witty, often action-packed account of Grimble's sojourn on the Gilberts, intermingled with accounts of the islanders' folklore and traditions. Arthur was a born raconteur, and the liveliness and sheer poetry of his descriptions found his books racing up the British best-seller lists. Then, for many years afterwards, they were avidly studied as part of the school English syllabus. In 1956, the first of the books was adapted as the British film *Pacific Destiny*, but it played fast and loose with the narrative, and ironed out the author's complex viewpoint on island life.

It was a time of much British colonial activity, with countries such as India, Kenya and Fiji opening up new horizons and opportunities abroad. Grimble certainly fed the romance of this surge although, if read closely, he did not intend to. In the opening of *Pattern* he notes, with tongue firmly in cheek: 'Dominion over palm and pine or whatever else happened to be noticeably far-flung was the heaven-sent privilege of the Bulldog Breed. Kipling had said so.' Arthur was (for the era) the kindly, acceptable, maverick face of imperialism. He was generous-hearted, had a flair for languages and a fascination for folklore. His friendliness and eventual ability to communicate fluently with his charges in their own language eventuated in him becoming the only white man initiated into various Gilbertese societies without marrying a native.

The Grimbles arrived first on Ocean Island, or Banaba, which the Pacific Islands Trading Company mined for phosphate. Here he was introduced to book-keeping, magistrate's sessions and a life which centred around the Residency, a spacious white wooden-frame bungalow which housed the resident commissioner — 'the Old Man'. There was even cricket, played against the islanders, who were mainly interested in the overtime this gave them as Company employees. Arthur, though, was touched and impressed primarily by the native villages of neatly arranged thatched huts on stilts, the flaming hibiscus, and the laughing, pareu-clad Banabans. His poet's ear also immediately fell in love with 'the music of the lovely island-names' — Butaritari, Tarawa, Abemama, Funafuti.

Grimble's anthropological interests and natural friendliness was soon stirred by the warmth and openness of the Banabans, and he learned much just by walking through their villages. The houses, made of plaited palm and pandanus leaves, were designed and placed so that screens could be drawn back to observe and communicate with neighbours and passers-by. 'If you wanted a silent and reflective stroll,' he wrote, 'you avoided a village, for it was almost beyond human power to resist the temptation of their charming and curious gossip.' In this way he met Tebutinnang, 'Movement of Clouds', a seven-year-old girl, naked apart from a garland of white flowers, who takes her place in a gallery of native portraits which Arthur drew with much warmth and skill. This diminutive teacher helped him with some of the difficulties of Gilbertese, as well as the finer points of native customs. It was from her that he learned the art of the appreciative post-dinner belch.

Grimble ('Kurimbo' to the islanders) was stationed on several of the group's beautiful atolls as district officer, and his three daughters were born on the islands. Upon his eventual return to England, the records he made of their life in the Pacific were turned into two best-selling books and various magazine articles which introduced the reader to a new world of vivid characters and easy-going, sun-soaked island life. The lonely atolls of the Gilbert and Ellice group have the unique distinction of straddling both the equator and the International Date Line. They have also been made distinguished by the writings of Arthur Grimble, a man who knew and loved them as no other visitor.

Between November 1916 and March 1917, William Somerset Maugham (1874–1965), one of the most versatile and popular authors of the century, toured the South Pacific with his secretary/lover, Gerald Haxton. In Hawaii, Samoa, Fiji, Tonga, Tahiti and Moorea, he did not so much seek the beauty of the islands ('Herman Melville and Pierre Loti had prepared me for that') but, rather, he looked for new characters and new stories to tell about them. At the time, he felt that he had exhausted Europe as a setting. In particular, he sought inspiration for an idea he had long cherished, a novel based on the life of the painter Paul Gauguin. What emerged was some of his very best writing — *The Moon and Sixpence* (1919), which was filmed in 1942, and a collection of seven short stories, among them the famous 'Rain'. From the latter emerged perhaps his most famous character, good-time gal Sadie Thompson, portrayed three times on celluloid by screen idols Joan Crawford, Gloria Swanson and Rita Hayworth.

Maugham's stories, like those of the Australian writer Louis Becke, were in the main unromantic, unheroic and concerned with the darker, lascivious side of paradise. Moral dilemmas have followed the white characters out to the islands, magnified by an oppressive heat which raises tempers and passions. The beautiful, languorous setting merely mocks this situation. Maugham points out: 'I did find real men and women in the islands of the South Pacific struggling against physical and moral decadence, unable to adjust themselves to the alien environment, in spite of its lush tropical beauty.' These 'real men and women' form the basis of stories such as 'Rain', 'Red', 'Mackintosh' and 'The Pool'. In 'Red', a native woman pines for a sailor whom she believes was press-ganged, but who has deserted her; 'Mackintosh' is the tale of a brutal island administrator locked in battle with his mild, educated assistant. Even more downbeat is 'The Pool', about a European who, while bathing, meets a lovely young Samoan girl, but then sinks into depression and alcoholism when he cannot make the cultural adjustments to live with her. This story may well have been intended as a satire on Loti's love for Rarahu.

The inspiration for 'Rain' came from a Miss Thompson from the red light district of Honolulu, who had the cabin next to Maugham's on a steamer bound for Pago Pago, American Samoa. She was heading south to seek her fortune however she might, and had begun by entertaining men in her cabin. She was 'plump, pretty in a coarse fashion, perhaps not more than twenty-seven', but she knew her business. She became the model for Maugham's Sadie, who used her wiles to gain the upper hand over her missionary persecutor. The setting for the story is the Pago Pago boarding house in which Maugham stayed with his secretary and lover Gerald Haxton, and which has now become Sadie's Restaurant, the best eating house in Pago Pago.

Willie and Gerald loved Tahiti. They pulled into Papeete harbour in Febuary 1917, and Maugham found the bright colourful mix of shops and neat, tree-shaded roads to have 'a subtly French character' which reminded him of a provincial town in Touraine. They stayed in the legendary Hotel Tiara, run by the half-white Louvaina Chapman, which was thinly disguised in *The Moon and Sixpence* as the Hotel de la Fleur, run by Tiara Johnson. (Brooke had stayed at the Tiara while recovering from coral poisoning.) While researching Gauguin's sojourns upon the island, Maugham came across a painted door, in the vicinity of Mataiea, which had been decorated by the painter in payment for being nursed back to health by the native owner of the house. Thinking quickly, Maugham offered 200 francs for the door. In 1962, he sold a panel from it at Sotheby's for $37,400.

In several ways, Maugham's stay on the islands very adequately recompensed the long journey involved. It released his writer's block with a vengeance, and he revealed to his fascinated readership the desperate, off-course losers who hide away, adrift, in the lapsed paradise of the South Seas. And no other writer, except perhaps Becke, could do this job as competently.

If London, Maugham and Loti had formed an unlikely alliance to produce a novel, they would have written the lives of Charles Bernard Nordhoff (1887–1947) and James Norman Hall (1887–1951). These two American writers, who visited the islands and stayed on, are known to the

Nordhoff and Hall at work in Hall's library at his home in Arue, Tahiti

novel-reading and movie-watching public as the creative team behind some of the best-loved romantic adventures of the Pacific. The trilogy *Mutiny on the Bounty* (1932), *Men Against the Sea* (1934) and *Pitcairn's Island* (1935) made their names synonymous with the South Sea swashbuckler, and five of their novels have been turned into movies — two of these more than once. For sheer romance, thrills and tragedy, however, the drama of their own lives, in their chosen home of Tahiti, came close to that of their books.

'Nordie' and James met during World War I in the famous Lafayette Flying Corps of the French Foreign Legion which, quite independently, they had decided to join for what glamour and thrills it might provide. By 1919, they made a pact to put civilization as far behind them as possible, Tahiti forming the focus of their daydreams. And the dream started just as soon as their ship approached the reef at Papeete, where they learned from the captain that the perfume which wafted across the water to greet them was a heady melange of frangipani, tiare tahiti and hinano flowers. Once ashore, without wasting a moment, they immediately began to comb French Polynesia for tales to sell to magazines back home, the *Atlantic Monthly* always being their main outlet.

Within a year, Nordie met Tua Tearae Smidt, a beautiful nineteen-year-old Tahitian who serenaded him with folk songs on their first date. They were married at the end of 1920, and built a home on a 50-acre (20-hectare) plot in the district of Punaauia. While his friend had settled down, however, James drifted and began to think that paradise could drive you mad with its indolence.

A typical Gilbertese village, Kiribati, very much as Arthur Grimble would have seen them when he lived on the islands

The island of Moorea at sunset, viewed across the Sea of the Moon,
from the estuary of the Punaruu River on the east coast of Tahiti. This spectacular sight,
akin to the mythical Bali-ha'i, has lured across practically every visiting writer

Na Pali coast, Kauai, used as a location in the films South Pacific *and* Blue Hawaii

Paul Theroux making the popular pilgrimage to Gauguin's grave on the Marquesan island of Hiva Oa

Two years later, at the age of thirty-eight, James joined his friend when he fell in love with the sixteen-year-old Sarah Terairei Winchester, daughter of a Tahitian woman and a white seaman. The Halls moved north of Papeete to the district of Arue, where they purchased a large hilltop frame house whose veranda looked out across Matavai Bay, where the ships of all the great explorers once anchored. Today, the house still stands, as a museum to the writer.

Nordhoff and Hall began to collaborate on books, dividing each project down the middle, then swapping contributions to revise each other's work. It was Hall's idea to combine their talents on the subject of the *Bounty* and her mutinous crew, a project requiring great research and careful period reconstruction. They solved the major problem of motivation by portraying, in a realistic style, the irresistible allure of Tahiti itself. The commercial success of the first episode led to the rest of the trilogy and several movie versions — although the two authors would only live to see the 1932 Australian version, with Errol Flynn, and the 1935 film, with Clark Gable. In general, no movie adaptation of their books pleased them.

The strain of the work, plus that infamous tropical affliction 'ennui', began to tell on Nordie. He was drinking too much, and when his fourth child and only son died suddenly, he withdrew and became depressive. The writing team continued, though with less input from Nordie. *Hurricane* (1936) was another best-seller, and the Dorothy Lamour movie, a year later, was a huge box-office hit. But as the partners continued to peddle the adventure and romance of Oceania, the real thing was relentlessly chipping away at the team mentally and physically. Nordie strayed from his wife, who in reaction took their Tahitian chauffeur as a lover. There was a scene with Nordie waving a pistol, though no shots were fired, and separation and heavier boozing followed. Then Hall caught elephantiasis (the enlargement of a limb, caused by the nematode worm) in one leg, from which he never really recovered.

The miracle is that, as matters got worse, the creative team somehow struggled on, even managing more best-sellers and movie spin-offs. But paradise was losing its bloom. Nordie died back in California from a heart attack, and Hall at his home on Tahiti, weak from fighting his illness. Both men had paid a high price for their years of tropical bliss, but their love affair with the islands, which they recorded so vividly in their books, seemed more than worth it at the time. Significantly, the plaque on Hall's Tahitian tomb quoted the opening lines of one of his early poems:

> *Look to the northward stranger*
> *Just over the hill there*
> *Have you in your travels seen*
> *A land more passing fair?*

The case of Zane Grey (1875–1939), who arrived on Tahiti five years after Nordhoff and Hall, is an intriguing one. Few would associate this hardy, old-style frontiersman — and author of such best-selling westerns as *Riders of the Purple Sage* (1912) — with the lazy, sensuous world of the South

Zane Grey (back left), *with friends and staff, at Flower Point camp, Vairao, on Tahiti's southern peninsular, circa 1928*

Seas. At first, Grey disapproved of what he saw. He disliked native 'promiscuity' and the 'depravity' of visiting Euopeans. He particularly disapproved of a people who seemed to occupy their time languidly sitting around. 'I did not wonder,' he complained, 'that Robert Louis Stevenson went to the South Seas a romancer and became a militant moralist.'

Grey first visited Tahiti in 1924, but his major stopovers on the island were in 1928 and 1930. He was an avid sightseer and game fisherman, and in 1928 built a fishing camp at Flower Point, Vairao, on the southern peninsula. The complex consisted of six cottages, a dining cabin, a cook house, an electricity plant and a wooden jetty built out over the lagoon. Nothing remains of the camp today, but its location is near to the marina of the Hotel Puunui.

During his time on Tahiti, Zane was a familiar figure to the tight little European community. Despite his disapproval of Papeete, he would frequent the famous club Cercle Bougainville, and became a companion of fellow novelist and fisherman Charles Nordhoff. Tales of his sporting prowess spread around the community like wildfire.

Slowly, the allure of Polynesia worked its way under Grey's tough, disapproving hide, until he was forced to admit to its charms. 'The enchantment of Tahiti never fully burst upon me until I returned to my camp at Flower Point, Vairao, early in March, 1930,' he wrote. From his developing love for the islands arose two books: *Tales of Tahitian Waters* (1931), which chronicles his time based at Flower Point, and *The Reef Girl*, one of his best novels and an altogether different affair.

Revealing just how profoundly the place had worked its spell, the novel is above all a celebration of Tahiti's beauty, and unashamedly erotic to boot. When *The Reef Girl* was submitted for publication shortly after Grey's death, it was rejected as being too 'daring' a book from such a writer. Amazingly, it wasn't until 1977 that the book finally appeared in print.

One of the latest literary visitors to Oceania is Paul Theroux. In the early 1990s, he roughly followed the ancient canoe migration route from Papua eastwards, through Melanesia, into Polynesia, then northwards to Hawaii, taking with him a collapsible kayak. While such a vessel may not measure up to Stevenson's *Casco* or London's *Snark*, the freedom such a boat afforded, and the opportunities for daredevilry, gave him the edge on more recent visitors to the area. He was able to come across more curious island characters than any writer since, perhaps, Louis Becke. His chronicle of this epic voyage is easily the equal of those other great literary accounts, Stevenson's *In the South Seas* and London's *The Cruise of the Snark*.

American-born but London-based, Theroux has become one of the most successful contemporary travel writers, establishing his reputation in 1975 with *The Great Railway Bazaar*. In the *Chicago Herald Tribune World*, it was once suggested that, 'With undisguised contempt for the people and customs of the countries he visits, with no sympathetic bonhomie, Theroux has a certain arrogant charm.' It was thus intriguing to see this charm at work on the South Seas.

Theroux's Pacific odyssey was an offshoot of a trip to Australasia to promote a previous book. The title, *The Happy Isles of Oceania*, is obviously ironic, as he paddles from isle to isle determined to find the seedy underside of the Pacific dream. He is, nevertheless, quite often overwhelmed by the beauty of the islands: 'And most of the night, under the brilliant half moon that lighted the starry sky and the jungle treetops and the high clouds breezing across it and made silhouettes of the coconut palms, the children sang and laughed, by the surge of the sloshing lagoon.' At moments like this, Theroux reminds one of Arthur Grimble's lyrical enthusiasm.

An original choice for his first stop was the Trobriands, for the purposes of checking out these Islands of Love, as they were called by anthropologist Bronislaw Malinowski (in his book *Argonauts of the Western Pacific*, 1922). Here he met his first contingent of 'troppo' (mad from the tropical heat) Australians, more of whom he would be running into on a regular basis throughout the islands. It was also his initiation into the cult of Spam, a tinned meat which, depressingly, seems central to the diets of so many Pacific islanders. Otherwise, 'the Trobes' were much as the great anthropologist had found them, with the same bands of female rapists operating during the annual yam festival, and the natives' continuing propensity for teasing strangers.

For a time, the village of Kaisiga, on the small island of Kaileuna, became a peaceful and friendly base from which Theroux explored in his kayak. He particularly enjoyed the way the Trobriand islanders had little sense of time and no idea of anyone's age. The atmosphere was shattered, however, by an unfortunate incident on one of his paddling expeditions. On an islolated waterway, Theroux found himself surrounded by a gang of aggressive adolescents wielding spears in a menacing manner. Certain that he would die, far from any help or witnesses, it was touch and go for one chilling moment, and not the kind of adventure he had hoped from the South Seas.

At Tonga, the kayak provided Theroux with the opportunity to indulge in the desert island experience. Heading south from the larger island of Vava'u, he came across Pau, a small, uninhabited isle with a coconut grove and sandy beach. Unpredictable everyday realities took some of the shine off the adventure: it rained a lot, he had forgotten matches and the fruit bats made a din all day. None the less, Paul paddled about contentedly, met 'the prettiest women I had ever seen in the Pacific', and encountered bad-tempered dogs that he hoped would end up as a local dish. In the end, boredom drove him on. As a parting shot, he created one of his infamous broadsides, inspired by his experience on the island of Tongatapu: 'Tongan snobbery, offensiveness, incivility and rampant xenophobia had kept the great glorious archipelago of Vava'u one of the least spoiled places in the Pacific.'

Although Theroux had no regard at all for Papeete, the bustling capital of Tahiti (no visiting writer, other than Maugham, has ever liked it), the nearby isle of Moorea gets the best rating of the trip thus far. In a rare moment of unguarded romanticism, he visits Moorea in much the same fashion as Loti, who had gone there to seek his brother's one-time Polynesian lover. Paul is seeking a Mimi Theroux, whom he has vaguely heard of, in the belief, like Loti, that he may have blood ties with the islands.

Loti did not find the woman he sought, but Theroux does. Mimi, who is Chinese with a touch of Polynesian, and whose room overlooks Cook's Bay (which Theroux finds 'one of the most beautiful spots in the whole of Oceania') was once married to a distant cousin of Paul's, a roving adventurer named James, with whom she sailed the seas for several years before they parted at Tahiti, the place where they had originally met. This episode in his book is conveyed in a quiet tone of contentment: a sublime mix of satisfaction at having discovering Mimi — his obscure family link with the islands — and the simple enjoyment of Moorea's peaceful beauty.

If he was touched by Moorea, Theroux goes 'troppo' for Hawaii. Kayaking along the spectacular Na Pali coast on the island of Kauai, he recalls myths ancient and modern about these huge, sheer bluffs. This is where the Hawaiian deity Pele fell in love with a mortal, and it was also the location for Bali-Ha'i in the film *South Pacific*. He is stung by the tentacle of a jellyfish, but nothing can diminish his rapture:

> *Even with my stinging arm in this choppy sea, I would rather be here among the cathedral-like contours of the cliffs on this high island than seeing its architectural equivalent in Europe — and I knew that the next time I saw Westminster Abbey or Notre Dame I would be instantly reminded of the soaring Na Pali coast and miss it terribly.*

That night, by the light of a camp fire on an isolated beach, he contemplates his odyssey: 'I had had some happy times paddling through the Pacific, but their origin had been sights and sounds. I had not experienced much comfort … But this was different, this was one of the most pleasant interludes in my trip.' At last, here in Hawaii, he has found a corner of paradise — albeit one under threat. Paradise is defined here as a place which has everything at once — physical beauty (where it has not been spoiled), a good climate, and 'great hospitals and schools and social services and stores'. Could the fact that Hawaii is very American also form part of Theroux's attraction?

Today, less fiction seems to flow from the pens of visitors to the islands. Travel narratives, with personal asides, seem the preferred format for writers such as Theroux. Two other notable examples of the form are Cherry Farrow's *Pacific Odyssey* (1990) and Julian Evans's *Transit of Venus* (1992). The trend seems to be, rather, towards indigenous Oceanic fiction. A fine introduction to this is *The Faber Book of Contemporary South Pacific Stories* (1994), a volume which points to the way ahead.

Margaret Mead in 1925, looking more than a little self-conscious in native Samoan costume

CHAPTER SIX

PARADISE UNDER THE MICROSCOPE

THE LAST OF the great oceans to be to be explored by Europeans, the Pacific was also the first to be subjected to methodical scientific examination. If the South Seas presented startling images of paradise to artists and writers, it presented a series of intellectual challenges to the natural historian and to the anthropologist. Exposure to the Pacific helped steer scientific thought along evolutionary lines and, strange as it seems, Oceanic social characteristics threw light upon our own cultural patterns.

From the fertile study-grounds of the South Pacific emerged several scientific celebrities. Their discoveries reached beyond the academic world to create mingled unease and delight about the wonders of Oceania. The earliest of these figures, Sir Joseph Banks, introduced an amazed English public to the white-robed Tahitian Omai; Charles Darwin outraged his generation by returning from Oceania to challenge traditional beliefs about the Creation; Bronislaw Malinowski provided a rather frank account of the islanders' sexual mores; Margaret Mead's studies of Samoa unleashed theories which overturned many cherished beliefs about the modern Western family; and Thor Heyerdahl appealed to everyone's sense of adventure and mystery when he set sail across the Pacific on his raft *Kon-Tiki*.

Captain Cook's first voyage was promoted by the Royal Society — Britain's oldest scientific institution, founded in 1660 — which encouraged the empirical scientific methods of keen observation, and the keeping of accurate records. The voyage of the *Endeavour* was planned as a scientific expedition. It included a team of trained, professional observers and artists, so that the ship resembled a floating laboratory. And at the centre of this scientific fraternity was the debonair twenty-four-year-old botanist Joseph Banks (1743–1820).

Banks was the son of a rich Lincolnshire landowner, and was thus able to perform the unusual action of funding Israel Lyons as Professor of Botany at Oxford in order to study under him. At the age of twenty-one he came into a huge inheritance which enabled him to travel, which he did more as an explorer than as a traditional dilettante. While most young English gentlemen undertook the fashionable, vaguely educational Grand Tour of Europe, Joseph instead horrified his relatives and friends by setting off in 1766 for the reputedly savage shores of Newfoundland and Labrador. Two years later, he was ready to attempt the even more hazardous venture of circumnavigating the world with Captain Cook. He would still not listen to advice about a spell in Europe: 'Every blockhead does that; my Grand Tour shall be one round the whole globe.'

With £10,000 — an enormous outlay for those days — he funded his own part in the voyage. He carefully selected an entourage of professionals: Swedish naturalist Daniel Carl Solander, artists Sydney Parkinson, John Reynolds and Alexander Buchan, and assistant draughtsman Herman Sporing. Besides which, he insisted on his two pet greyhounds coming along, sharing his private deck cabin and personal supply of victuals.

On Tahiti, Banks co-ordinated the team, took notes and samples of flora and fauna, and learned what he could of the language. He possessed the additional skills of a born mediator, and was frequently called upon to arbitrate between Cook and the islanders over matters of theft. He would regularly eat and sleep out under the stars with the Tahitians and, being a personable young man, found himself a willing favourite with the women: 'The ladies ... showed us all kinds of civilities our situation could admit of.' For the entire three months of their stay on the island, he also found himself the unwilling victim of the lascivious advances of the well-rounded Queen Oberea. So determined was she to seduce Banks that during one camping trip she hid his clothes after he had undressed for the night, ensuring his helplessness against her overtures.

Back home, the press unfairly caricatured him as 'Voyager, Monster-hunter and Amoroso', conveniently ignoring the fact that he left Tahiti in possession of a remarkably comprehensive collection of both naturalist and anthropological importance. Not only did he record a great deal of the flora and fauna of Tahiti, but he exceeded his brief and drew up a catalogue of the islanders' social, religious and political structures, together with a working Polynesian vocabulary. He was particularly proud of the fact that he had even learned the art of peeling a green coconut with his teeth.

Needless to say, the young man was literally able to dine out on all this for a considerable time after his return home. Rich, tall, handsome, bronzed by the tropic sun, Banks was the much-prized guest of honour at any number of society dinner parties, where his tales of Oceanic wonders held glittering socialites spellbound. Often accompanying him at such events would be a sample from his huge collection of plants, animals and birds, insects, shells, minerals and native artifacts. He even introduced his collection to King George III, who became his lifelong friend.

Banks's links with the South Pacific did not end here. In 1773, he was appointed special advisor and director of the Royal Gardens at Kew. In this capacity he was asked by the government to draw up instructions for the collecting team aboard the infamous *Bounty*. It was their duty to take young breadfruit plants from Tahiti to the West Indies, where they would be needed to help feed the huge numbers of slaves labouring on the sugar plantations. Banks's instructions, which paid no mind to the sailors (let alone the slaves), included taking up much of the cramped ship's quarters with 1,000 saplings, then compounding the error by short-rationing the water in order to keep the plants happy. Some historians believe that this situation could well have been the last straw that led to the legendary mutiny.

The botanist's other encounter with the islands came about when Cook's second voyage to the Pacific returned with the live trophy of a young Tahitian man named Omai. Since Banks was familiar with the young man's tongue, he was enlisted to look after Omai during his sojourn in England. Omai's personable nature overwhelmed London society, and he was shown off everywhere. At Lord Sandwich's country residence, the Tahitian delighted a gathering by cooking a shoulder of mutton, native-style, in an earth oven. His portrait was painted by such fashionable artists as Joshua Reynolds, William Parry and Nathaniel Dance. And when he met the King, it was widely reported to an amused readership that he fell to his knees and announced, 'How do, King Tosh!' ('Tosh' being his version of George). He was always charming, meticulous in appearance and friendly, making such an agreeable impression that he inspired a play at Covent Garden, *Omai: Or a Trip Round the World* (1785).

Towards the end of Omai's stay, there were various complaints that Banks had done nothing much to enlighten the Tahitian, having merely shown him off. However, this ignored the fact that Omai had picked up much along the way without being schooled, and that what he had learned of civilized ways drove a wedge between himself and his people when he went back to them. He died shortly after his return to the islands from some unknown illness. As for Banks, when he died in 1820, the great man had assigned no one to carry on his work. Furthermore, he left no important published works, and his papers and letters were auctioned off to autograph dealers and scattered around the world. None the less, his many personal achievements, including his role as scientific promoter of the South Seas, had ensured his place in history.

Most eighteenth-century biologists would relate their findings to a view of nature often referred to as the 'great chain of universal being'. This meant that each particular form of life on earth passes on its likeness to its offspring, so that these forms are perpetuated from the beginning to the very end of the world. This static model of nature did not seem tenable, however, to scientists who came to the Pacific, and were faced with what seemed to be new types of familiar species. In the first half of the nineteenth century, three scientists — Charles Robert Darwin, Joseph Dalton Hooker and Thomas Henry Huxley — came to the Pacific and stumbled upon evidence that jointly suggested an alternative history of life on earth, one involving a new picture of dynamic evolution.

The work of Hooker and Huxley helped confirm the theories of Darwin, just as each of the men acted as champions for the great naturalist's much-attacked opinions. Hooker (1817–1911), a botanist, was the first of the three men to visit the Pacific, arriving there in 1839 on HMS *Erebus*, in the post of assistant surgeon and naturalist. Visiting Tasmania, New Zealand and some of the islands within the vicinity, he returned with specimens, sketches and detailed notes on a variety of plants and their resemblances. Six years later, Huxley (1825–95) came to the region on board HMS *Rattlesnake*, again as naturalist and ship's surgeon. As the *Rattlesnake* surveyed the Torres Straits between north Australia and Papua New Guinea with only the most makeshift equipment, Huxley studied and classified jellyfish. His major findings, like those of Hooker, only became obvious after the proposals of Darwin were announced. Huxley, though, is most famous for being Darwin's chief advocate and defender at public debates. Both these men, however, were quite overshadowed by the Oceanic discoveries of one of the greatest naturalists of all.

Charles Darwin (1809–82), the son of a Shrewsbury physician, spent most of his time as a schoolboy fooling about in the chemistry lab, and loved nothing more than hunting and shooting in the woods around his home. Both his headmaster and father thought him a disgrace and a wastrel. Later, at Edinburgh University, he studied medicine until, in 1827, he attended an operation without anaesthetics and rushed from the theatre in horror, vowing that a medical career was not for him. Taking his errant son in hand, his father next sent Charles to Cambridge to prepare him for entry to the Church of England as a clergyman. This seemed the final chance for Charles actually to do something worthwhile with his life. Nothing, however, could have been further from his future social role because at Cambridge Charles met John Henslow, who fired him with a passionate interest in natural history. After gaining a poor degree in 1831, Darwin accepted an offer from Henslow to sail on an Admiralty survey voyage as an unpaid naturalist. Under the command of Robert FitzRoy, HMS *Beagle*, a ten-gun brig, was to cruise the coast of South America, then continue across the South Seas on mainly meteorological assignments.

The five years of this voyage proved the most important period in the young man's life and in the history of the biological sciences. Not only was Darwin enthralled by the trip ('It shall be as a birthday for the rest of my life'), it helped him forge the scientific tools with which he would alter for ever our view of life on earth. When he embarked upon the voyage he did so with no formal scientific training, but by the time he returned he had taught himself empirical methods whereby he would go on to make his mark on the whole history of thought.

In Darwin's thoroughly entertaining account of his expedition, *The Voyage of the Beagle* (1845), he goes beyond mere scientific description, even indulging occasionally in a little humour and poetic scene-setting. As someone only accustomed to the English landscape, he points out how 'even the novel aspect of an utterly sterile land possesses a grandeur which more vegetation might spoil'. Thus it is that when he came across the Galapagos Islands he was entranced by 'the strange Cyclopean scene' of a couple of 200-pound (90-kilogram) tortoises: 'These huge reptiles, surrounded by the black lava, the leafless shrubs, and large cacti, seemed to my fancy like some antediluvian animals.' Yet it was some altogether different creatures on this archipelago which were to provide the building blocks for his subversive theory of evolution and natural selection.

He came across 'a most singular group of finches' which differed from one island to the next. Some ate insects, others seeds, and their sizes and bills varied in relation to diet and mode of life. Within only a few months after his return to England, Charles began to draw together his thoughts about this phenomenon: 'Animals, our fellow brethren in pain, disease, death, suffering and famine — our slaves in the most laborious works, our companions in our amusements — they may partake of our origin in one common ancestor — we may be all netted together.' And so it was that his experience of the South Pacific made Darwin aware that the scriptures did not present a literal guide to the history of man. From someone who had once set his mind on a career in the Church, he became an agnostic, believing that, since creation, all life has undergone adaptation to environment.

Darwin's further experiences of the South Seas did not generate anything else as profound as this. Unlike Banks, that jack-of-all-trades, Darwin took no particular interest in the culture of the islanders, although in the case of the Polynesians he was stimulated by his contact with them. After the Galapagos Islands, the *Beagle* sailed on to Tahiti, which Charles found the most sublime, if not the most scientifically stimulating, port of call. His reaction was not unlike that of most visitors: 'Tahiti, an island which must forever remain classical to the voyager in the South Sea.' He was struck by the beautiful reefs and verdure-clad hills, but he 'was pleased with nothing so much as with the inhabitants'. He found them intelligent, and thought their complexion made his skin seem 'like a plant bleached by the gardener's art'. Rather like Gauguin, however, the young man 'was much disappointed in the personal appearance of the women: they are far inferior in every respect to the men'.

He concluded his brief stay upon the island with a three-day trip inland to the mountains, in the company of native f: ⌐ds and guides. From this vantage point he was able to see and describe beautifully the sister island of Eimeo (Moorea): 'On the lofty and broken pinnacles, white massive clouds were piled up, which formed an island in the blue sky, as Eimeo itself did in the blue ocean.' He was also able to reflect briefly on the lot of the islander when he offered his friends a flask of spirits, which their dread of the missionaries made them sip only with great guilt. Darwin, however, did not agree with commentators such as Melville or Kotzebue, who found the islanders crushed and demoralized by the bullying missionaries. He found them instead happy and contented.

Darwin's view of Tahiti may well have been founded on the rather unscientific evidence of a short stay, but he would spend over twenty years refining his theory of evolution. And, like most good ideas, it was startlingly simple ('How extremely stupid not to have thought of that,' remarked Huxley). However, the voyage which brought him to his momentous conclusions also brought about his untimely demise. It is now reckoned that the mysterious illness which restricted his life for many years, and weakened his health severely, was caused by a parasite, probably picked up in South America. Ironically, Darwin's voyage was both a momentous event and a terrible curse.

All the early circumnavigators took some note of native culture and language, and sketches and paintings of ethnographic articles ensured some idea of South Sea life. But overall anthropological notions of Oceania remained crudely moralistic or romantic. The peoples of the South Seas were usually divided up between the 'hard primitives' (basically those of Australasia and Melanesia) and 'soft primitives' (Polynesia). Some believed that in Oceania we can see ourselves in our earlier nobility, and others that the South Pacific was the cradle for a new, greater civilization. Yet another theory held that the Marquesans were degenerate ancestors of an ancient Mexican empire. In this way, Western opinions swung between a consideration of the islanders as noble or ignoble, according to fashion.

Legitimate social anthropology did not develop until the second half of the nineteenth century, after the impact of Darwin. And one of the founding heroes of modern anthropology was the Polish-born Bronislaw Malinowski. Both he and Margaret Mead (one of the most popular of all anthropologists) made their names and built their careers upon their studies of the Pacific islanders.

Malinowski (1884–1942) undertook the most important anthropological work in the South Seas, though not the best publicized. A thin, scholarly-looking man, with an impressive domed forehead, he appeared to be the last person to be interested in the colourful sex lives of South Sea islanders. In 1914, he moved to London, where he worked for the British Museum and the London School of Economics. The same year, he set out on his first expedition, which would involve fieldwork on Papua New Guinea and the nearby Trobriand Islands for most of the next four years.

Malinowski put the Trobriands on the map for academics and the general public because he christened them, seductively, the Islands of Love. These low-lying coral islands, whose inhabitants have certain Polynesian characteristics, are the most interesting group in the Milne Bay area, in the east of Papua. Although the scientist's name is now freely associated with these islands, it was only a happy accident that Malinowski went there in the first place. When World War I broke out, the Australian authorities offered him the choice either of a safe harbour on their mainland, or of secretion upon the remote Trobriands. He chose the latter, and the rest is popular (and academic) history.

Malinowski set future anthropological trends for hands-on fieldwork. By living with his subjects, and joining in their day-to-day routines, he was able to separate ideal norms from actual behaviour. From this research came forth books with such arresting titles as *Argonauts of the South Pacific* (1922) and *The Sexual Life of Savages in North-Western Melanesia* (1929). The latter attracted great interest with its detailed, graphic descriptions of various acts, as well as for the listing of a startlingly wide native sexual vocabulary. In particular, he revealed a strange tradition, still practised, at yam harvesting. During this period, from roughly June to August, it is not unknown for some women in the south of the main island to capture and gang-rape passing men — not, apparently, a consummation devoutly to be wished for by the terrorized males of the district. Like all such passages in the book, Malinowski conveys these matters in a style which combines scientific detail with astonished, though restrained, period disapproval. Needless to say, on the practice of male rape, Malinowski was not willing to risk his own honour in order to bear scientific witness. 'I am unable to add those necessary touches of life which depend on actual observation,' he states matter-of-factly.

Malinowski, talking to a sorcerer, in the Trobriands, circa 1915

What serves to give more depth to these studies was a controversial, posthumously published volume of Malinowski's confessions, *A Diary in the Strict Sense of the Term* (1967). Here we are vouchsafed the strains, annoyances and insecurities of this style of isolated fieldwork, for after a day of the islanders' child-like teasing and lying, Malinowski would retire to his tent and vent his spleen in a notebook. It is intriguing to see the objective scientist reacting as an individual.

Throughout his career, Malinowski would constantly refer back to his extensive research of the South Seas. He was a prolific writer, whose books were translated into many languages, and who wrote the *Encyclopaedia Britannica*'s section on marriage, kinship and social anthropology. Malinowski did not, however, become as celebrated a public figure as Margaret Mead. It was left to her to popularize anthropology, as well as the islands of the Pacific, which provided her fieldwork locations.

Diminutive of stature, from a sheltered American middle-class background, Margaret Mead (1901–78) at first seems an unlikely figure to have undertaken a solo expedition in the 1920s to a remote part of the South Pacific. Her mother, however, was surprisingly forward-thinking for her time, taking up such unfashionable causes as the rights of blacks and women. Something of this campaigning ardour rubbed off on to her daughter, who in later years was to challenge many of the cultural preconceptions of modern American society. The groundwork for many of these revolutionary ideas came from a six-month stay on a Samoan island.

At Columbia University Margaret had studied the way in which civilization was encroaching upon Polynesian society in the Pacific, and she expressed the wish to travel to the region to investigate the phenomenon first-hand. Her lecturer, Professor Franz Boas, head of the Department of Anthropology, was horrified at the idea of a young woman engaging in such a risky undertaking. What was wrong with studying the American Indians? But Margaret wanted a less spoiled culture to study, so a compromise was reached. He ruled out the Tuamotus, where she wanted to go, and settled instead on American Samoa, where help and communication were easily and swiftly at hand. He also advised her to concentrate on the subject of adolescence, which was as hotly debated then as it is today.

When she arrived at Pago Pago on Tutuila Island in 1925, Margaret looked in vain for a village where traditional ways were paramount. Everywhere, American culture was permeating fast — from the food eaten to the clothes worn. Finally, she was obliged to travel about 100 miles (160 kilometres) from Tutuila, the main island of American Samoa, eastwards to T'au, in the Manu'a group. Here, in the tiny village of Luma, she found all she required for her fieldwork. She lived in the spare room of a wooden colonial-style house occupied by the family of Edward Holt, a US naval officer in charge of a dispensary. Near by was a small empty house where she could interview girls from the four island villages.

Margaret had briefly familiarized herself with the Samoan language before leaving Tutuila, and now set out to meet the families of Ta'u. Soon, she learned that her working relationship with them would have to involve a ritual exchange. She met, talked to the islanders and obtained information by sitting down with them, accepting shells and flowers and offering them paper, needles and thread, and other items useful to them. She would also write letters for them, photograph them and shop for them at the Navy store. Meanwhile, interviews with teenage girls continued at the spare house and on the veranda of the dispensary. She asked the girls about their family life, everyday experiences, and tested their intelligence. After six months, she returned to the States.

The publisher William Morrow accepted *Coming of Age in Samoa* on the condition that Margaret added an extra chapter relating her findings to the rebellious youth of America. The book was published in 1928 and was an instant best-seller, and a second printing followed immediately. It was given the professional seal of approval by none other than Malinowski, who decided it was an 'outstanding achievement'. But, more importantly, it turned out to be one of the most popular ever anthropology books with the general public, making people as aware of the discipline itself as of the exotic islands to which it introduced them.

Part of this enormous appeal lay in the final chapter requested by the publisher, linking a South Sea culture to matters at home. But Mead's writing had literary merit in its own right, and her ability to convey the picturesque, dreamy torpor of the South Seas is always present:

As the dawn begins to fall among the soft brown roofs and the slender palm trees stand out against a colorless, gleaming sea, lovers slip home from trysts beneath the palm trees or in the shadow of beached canoes, that the light may find each sleeper in his appointed place.

Here, on the very first page, the author whets our appetites by painting a romantic, impressionistic picture of the typical South Sea scene, while introducing the tantalizing subject of sex and the single Samoan.

If for no other reason, people were intrigued to read the book because there were those who were outraged by its apparent assumptions. Mead seemed to be hitting the ideal American family below the belt. Here she was pointing out that Samoans were so laid back, without any contemporary Western hang-ups, because they were raised by huge extended families. Maybe our isolated little nuclear families were too neurotically turned in upon themselves? Perhaps the Samoan's looser, wider group of surrogate parents can overcome the built-in problems of individual parenting — such as possessiveness? And where there was no possessiveness, sexual favours could be spread about with far greater impunity. Could this be a healthier situation than the guilt and jealousy which so often accompanies erotic adventure in Western societies? The impression given was that, while we struggled under the weight of our attitudes, adolescent Samoans were enjoying assorted pre-nuptial bliss beneath the palms.

Mead may not have single-handedly introduced the permissive society, but she certainly provided some of its foundations. In so doing, inevitably she laid herself open to personal and

The naval medical dispensary on the Samoan island of T'au, in which Margaret Mead lived during her fieldwork in 1925

professional criticism. Risibly, some argued that a woman who, although married, retained her maiden name (even her husband at the time use to call her 'Mr Mead') should not be listened to. Professionally, she would eventually be castigated for the incompleteness of her work on Ta'u: she had drawn too many conclusions from the evidence. The truth is that Margaret had worked with what material she was allowed to gather. As a woman, she was forbidden to attend certain all-male discussions on Samoa's political, religious and economic affairs. Therefore, while she had studied the family and the adolescent female, she could not put her findings within the context of the wider community.

Margaret returned to the Pacific in 1928, where she studied the tribes on Manus, the largest of the Admiralty Islands, off the north-east coast of Papua. From this arose her second book, *Growing Up in New Guinea* (1929). Her books, TV and radio interviews would continue to garner attention and controversy, but never again would her attack upon the American home and psyche seem quite so incisive. Looking back in later years, Mead also admitted that her Samoan idyll represented the happiest, most peaceful episode in her life.

The account so far of the scientist in the Pacific has its unlikely side. How is it possible that the remote, 'uncivilized' shores of the South Pacific could have attracted an eighteenth-century gentleman botanist, a man who could not stand the sight of blood, an insecure academic and a middle-class young woman out to seek evidence for her university thesis? Enter the handsome, dashing, sandy-haired Norwegian Thor Heyerdahl. Impossibly wholesome and hearty, Thor (named after the Scandinavian god of thunder) was born in 1914 in Larvik, and developed into an outward-bound, orienteering sort of adolescent after deep discussions with a rather philosophical local hermit. At this time, Thor could frequently be seen skiing bare-chested, and looking as if he could well have survived in the frozen wastes of a Jack London novel or journeyed to the centre of the earth in a book by Jules Verne. He developed the position that modern man was too much the armchair intellectual and had reduced his powers of direct observation. Advocating a return to nature, he dreamed of tropical locations where one would only need instinct to survive. Studying zoology at Oslo University in 1933, he met the fetching Liv Torp, a young lady who shared his romantic dreams. They were married in 1936, and the very next day set off for the South Seas, financed by Thor's father.

On the Marquesan island of Fatu Hiva, the Heyerdahls reverted to an Adam and Eve existence. Heading into the fabulous valley of Omoa, with the help of friendly locals they built a house of plaited bamboo, with a roof of woven coconut palm leaves. They flung aside their clothes, washed in the river and lived mainly on fruit from the surrounding trees. Thor wrote that, 'Rather than feeling poor and naked, we felt rich as if wrapped in the whole universe.' It was certainly no regular honeymoon. Thor scoured the forest for his expanding zoological collection and grew interested in various archaeological remains — skulls, terraces, stone giants. He began to muse upon the problems of how the Polynesians had arrived there so long ago, and from where they had come. During their year on the Marquesas, Thor's interest shifted from zoology to anthropology.

Portrait of Darwin at age thirty-one, by George Richmond, circa 1839. His highly formative trip to the South Seas
'shall be as a birthday for the rest of my life', he wrote

From left to right: *Omai, live Tahitian trophy, his host Sir Joseph Banks, and Swedish naturalist Dr Carl Solander*

Thor Heyerdahl studies the impressive statues of Easter Island before drawing all the wrong conclusions

Several of the islands bear monuments to the war fought in the Pacific. Here, in Kiribati, a fighter plane rusts rather romantically beneath a palm, beside a lagoon

Hawaiian actor Jason Scott Lee scales the cliffs of Easter Island's vast crater in the movie Rapa Nui *(1994), a film about the island's tumultuous history*

He became particularly fascinated by the myths about the Polynesian hero Tiki, 'Son of the Sun', who closely resembled a legendary pre-Inca hero of South America.

As for the back-to-nature experiment, the couple were grateful for the experience, but the vicissitudes involved — particularly the dreariness of the Marquesan winter, during which they developed terrible leg ulcers — led them to conclude that all roads lead onwards, not back. Modern man must now look for nature inside himself; there was nowhere else to turn. The real achievement of the voyage had been its inspiration for Heyerdahl's burgeoning theory on the origins of the Polynesians. Prevailing ethnological opinion, then as now, was that the islanders migrated largely from Asia. On the basis of the Peruvian legend of Kon-Tiki, and the similarity of the stone statues of Easter Island and Peru, Thor developed the heretical view that, at least in part, the islands had been settled by prehistoric South Americans. Yet when he tried to publish these theories, their subversive nature led to doors slamming in his face. There was nothing for it — he would just have to go ahead and prove by his own example that such a Pacific voyage was possible. It became, indeed, a matter of professional and personal pride that he should succeed in this undertaking.

With tremendous willpower, Thor raised the funding for the voyage, and commissioned the construction of a special South American-style balsa-log raft. Accompanied by five friends — Knut Haugland, Erik Hesselberg, Torstein Raaby, Herman Waltzinger and Bengt Danielson — the *Kon-Tiki* set sail on April 28th 1947 from the coast of Peru. During the voyage, the crew performed various practical tasks: collecting meteorological and oceanographic data, testing radio and life-saving equipment for the British and American armed forces, eating experimental food rations, and filming the journey throughout. After drifting 4,300 miles (6,920 kilometres) for 101 days, the *Kon-Tiki* crashed on to the reef of Raroia in the Tuamotus, south of the Marquesas, and the crew waded ashore safe and sound. Part scientific experiment, mainly *Boys' Own* escapade, the voyage was completed as planned.

The expedition was not, however, the scientific triumph Heyerdahl had envisaged. To this day, the pundits of the anthropological establishment still only concede that some insigificant movement took place between prehistoric South America and Polynesia. In every other way, however, Thor was delighted. With the dark spectre of World War II still lingering in their minds, the general public took to the *Kon-Tiki* enterprise as a welcome diversion. Here was an inspiring, romantic, true-life adventure tale with a happy ending and an exotic location. School children (and most of their parents) took Thor and his crew to their hearts. His lively account of the voyage, *The Kon-Tiki Expedition* (1950), became an international best-seller, being translated into sixty-two languages and selling well over twenty million copies. It was even studied in schools. Thor also scored another hit with his film *Kon-Tiki*, which won the Oscar for Best Documentary Feature in 1951. From 1948 to 1952, in Europe and the United States, he lectured and talked extensively on radio and TV. In 1949, together with Knut Haugland, Heyerdahl founded the Kon-Tiki Museum in Oslo.

The Kon-Tiki phenomenon was so huge (in part, due to its timing) that its glory proved unrepeatable. Heyerdahl obtained much mileage from its success, managing to fund voyages across

A scantily clad Thor Heyerdahl and Liv Torp pretend to be Adam and Eve on the Marquesan island of Fatu Hiva in 1936

the other great oceans with the reed ships *Ra*, *Ra II* and *Tigris*. He has, however, never been as influential or as popular again, despite a host of books, articles, papers and TV programmes. Thor will doubtless be remembered primarily as an adventurer — in the mould of such twentieth-century figures as Cousteau, Scott and Fiennes — for in Heyerdahl was found a daredevil, roistering, real-life post-war hero equal to the challenge of the South Seas. He now lives where he believes the migration to Polynesia began. At Tucume, in north-west Peru, he has built a traditional adobe-brick house and called it, nostalgically, Casa Kon-Tiki.

One of the awe-inspiring 'manaebaes', or traditional village meeting houses, of the Kiribati Islands. In his capacity as amateur anthropologist, Arthur Grimble wrote of their importance to the group's social life

Jean Simmons, in sarong and hibiscus, for the 1949 version of The Blue Lagoon

CHAPTER SEVEN

SOUTH PACIFIC,

THE MOVIE

THE SOUTH PACIFIC has many dramas: the exploits of intrepid missionaries and explorers, romantic intrigue, slave-trading, piracy, cannibals, castaways, World War II invasion — to mention just the obvious. It has attracted its fair share of writers for the fresh themes and characters it can offer. But there is also the not inconsiderable matter of the region's spectacular visual appeal. Add these two aspects together and you have the prime ingredients for any number of movies — a state of affairs which Hollywood was not slow to exploit. Since the twenties, even before the movies talked, audiences have been tantalised by a panorama of palm trees, lagoons and sarong-clad sirens projected before them in the darkness. Through the popular medium of cinema, the many tales of the South Pacific have been spread to huge audiences all around the globe.

One of the earliest Oceanic movies is the silent production of Henry de Vere Stacpoole's 1908 novel *The Blue Lagoon* (1923). Made in Australia, it has seldom been seen elsewhere. There are, however, two other popular versions of the story — a wonderful British film made in 1948, and a 1980 Hollywood production which acquits itself rather well. *Return to the Blue Lagoon*, an ill-conceived Hollywood sequel committed in 1990, is probably best forgotten.

The reason for the regular reappearance of this story on the big screen may at first seem mysterious. The original novel is out of print almost everywhere, due mainly to various dated aspects of style. Not even the success of the 1980 film brought it back on to book-shop shelves. Nevertheless, the tale distills the romantic essence of the South Seas: Boy gets to know Girl on desert island teeming with fruit, fish and fresh water. The potential is there for the picturesque spectacle of underwater photography, scantily-clad protagonists, seascapes, landscapes, flora and fauna. There is also the compelling 'nature or nurture' theme, treated here with more sophistication than in Ballantyne's somewhat naïve *Coral Island*. (Indeed, one of the problems with the original novel of *The Blue Lagoon* is that it is too adult for children and too ingenuous for grownups.) Primarily, though, the enduring attraction of the story lies in the theme of (accidental) return to simplicity. Thrown back upon unadorned nature, the characters are freer to discover the fundamental constituents of life. This is the age-old appeal of the castaway plot.

Although the book's action is placed roughly in the Tuamotu Archipelago, north-east of Tahiti, the three later films were shot in Fiji, which has proved to be the most popular South Sea movie location after Hawaii — the closest to Hollywood. The cameras actually rolled upon the shores of Turtle Island (traditionally known as Nanuya Levu), which has been owned since 1972 by American drop-out Richard Evanson. As a result, Mr Evanson's island has had more fame bestowed upon it, for while it would be true to say that, beside the wiles and glamour of Jean Simmons in the 1948 version (also filmed there), and Brooke Shields in the 1980 remake, the beguiling beauty of Turtle Island has assumed its own star status. Trading on its romantic associations, the owner has turned it into an exclusive resort for well-heeled dreamers.

The American 'father of the documentary', Robert J. Flaherty, spent several years in Polynesia making three films. The best of them was the dramatised documentary *Moana* (1924), set on the Samoan island of Savai'i. The biggest problem Flaherty, the storyteller, came across while in the South Seas, was discovering a lack of real drama in the people's day-to-day lives. Having previously made *Nanook of the North*, a popular and innovative Eskimo drama, he had come to expect that where Western industrial civilization did not exist, there must be a heroic struggle with Nature. But the seas around Savai'i are more like a well-heated swimming pool, doubling as a larder, than an implacable enemy. Even 'farming', as such, did not exist on these fortunate islands. Indeed, there was more drama going on around the production than in it, especially Flaherty's confrontations with aggressive local German traders. The film turned out to be a modest success, and has a glowing beauty which makes one completely forget that it is not in colour. Paramount, however, were so unsure of how to promote it that they gave it the unlikely title *The Love Life of a South Sea Siren* and put fake palm trees across the facade of the Rialto on Broadway, which quickly gathered winter snow. On the strength of this small triumph, Flaherty then filmed Frederick O'Brien's *White Shadows in the South Seas* (1927). His most commercially successful South Seas project, though, was *Tabu* (1928), filmed on Tahiti. Neither of these two movies, however, could hold an usherette's torch to the splendours of *Moana*.

Like *Mutiny on the Bounty* and *The Blue Lagoon*, Somerset Maugham's most popular story, 'Rain', has taken up quite a bit of celluloid. Based on a character the author met in Pago Pago, American Samoa, it is the steamy drama of a prostitute and her missionary persecutor. (Such fire-and-brimstone missionaries also cropped up in the movies *Return to Paradise*, 1953, and *Hawaii*, 1966.) This classic confrontation between a man of God and a woman of the flesh, with its torrid island setting, makes for good visual drama. It was even adapted for the stage, when the legendary American actress Jeanne Eagels played Sadie in an extremely successful 1922 New York production. Even so, Hollywood diluted the biting tone of Maugham's original story, which cynically revealed the man beneath the cloth and the ultimate, ugly triumph of instinct. Hollywood was merely interested, as ever, in a vague connection between carnality and climate.

The meaty role of the harassed heroine has attracted actresses of the calibre of Gloria Swanson, Joan Crawford and Rita Hayworth — all flashing teeth and wild tresses. Gloria Swanson's *Sadie Thompson* (1928) was the earliest adaptation, but its being silent in no way diminishes its vigour, even though it can be a little stagey. *Rain* (1932), with Joan Crawford, gains greatly by location shooting on Catalina Island, and features the formidable lady in bangles and fish-net stockings. Despite the cop-out of a happy ending, Crawford is quite magnificent, though she was apparently terrified of the role, feeling her attempts were haunted by the classic interpretations of Eagels and Swanson. Rita Hayworth also acquits herself well with a provocative performance in *Miss Sadie Thompson* (1953), and adds a few songs to give the tale an unexpected musical dimension. Song titles such as 'Hear No Evil, See No Evil' tend, however, to provide a rather broad parody of the drama. (Indeed, as unlikely as it seems, in 1944, Maugham's blistering South Sea tale was staged as a Broadway musical, starring June Havoc, with numbers by Vernon Duke.) This fifties version was the only one which was actually filmed on the islands — in this case Hawaii — and, as bizarre as it seems, was originally shot in 3-D. This system is employed to erotic effect in the number 'The Heat is On', where the redoubtable Miss Hayworth performs a sweaty dance routine for some astonished marines. Not as subtle as Maugham, perhaps, but it does rather neatly encapsulate Hollywood's notion of South Seas' steamy sexuality.

Maugham's savagely brilliant novel *The Moon and Sixpence*, based on Gauguin's life on Tahiti, was also committed to celluloid in 1942, with a magnificent performance by George Sanders. A stylish and fairly faithful adaptation, the movie was very much the product of its director–screenwriter–producer Albert Lewin, a man whose pre-Hollywood career included the jobs of lecturer and drama critic. Even so, the truth of Gauguin's venereal disease was too strong for United Artists, who had the painter die of leprosy, and then went briskly into colour for a concluding close-up of some of his paintings.

Nordhoff and Hall's *Mutiny on the Bounty* (1932), closely based on the historical tale of Captain Bligh's mutineers upon Tahiti, became a best-selling novel with its mix of action and romance in an exotic setting. The central drama of *Mutiny* is that of a shipful of frustrated, bored eighteenth-century Englishmen falling under the irresistible spell of a South Pacific island. This is still very strong stuff. It was first filmed as *In the Wake of the Bounty* (1930), an Australian semi-documentary never seen outside its country of origin, and featuring a twenty-four-year-old Tasmanian named Errol Flynn. Made on a shoestring budget by one Charles Chauvel, it actually featured underwater footage of the remains of the *Bounty* in shallow water off Pitcairn Island. The film, however, was bought up by MGM to keep it off the American market. Clips from it eventually appeared in promotional material for the studio's own 1935 version of the tale.

The roistering, mutineering hero, Fletcher Christian, has actually attracted several big-name stars. Besides Flynn (who was not famous at the time), we have Clark Gable (1935), Marlon Brando (1962) and Mel Gibson (1984). (Perhaps we should also include pop pin-up David Essex, who played Christian in his 1983 London stage musical *Mutiny!*) Only Brando did his homework and, while the others used the opportunity to further their dashing screen images, he played Christian as a dandified fop. Gable, in particular, balked at the notion of shaving off his moustache and sporting stockings and a pigtail. Brando and Gibson, however, were not at all averse to being seen succumbing to all that voluptuous tropical allure, and there is much location footage of them doing so. Not for Gable, though, the unmanly pareu or jaunty hibiscus behind the ear.

Only Brando stayed on in the islands, making a home, and bolt-hole, on the atoll of Tetiaroa (which he still owns), north of Tahiti, and having a long-standing affair with his leading lady, the Tahitian beauty Tarita Teriipia (whom he still sees). Indeed, the link between Brando and Tahiti was once as strong as that forged between Presley and Hawaii — a romantic connection seen both on the big screen and in the pages of fanzines. In both cases, the glamour of stardom was intoxicatingly superimposed on to the magic of the South Seas. Besides which, there was the seductive fantasy of escape to simplicity. Through Presley and Brando's dissatisfaction with the phoney glamour, frustrations and back-stabbing of Hollywood, we could vicariously flee with them to a South Sea island to enjoy a more back-to-basics life in the sun.

Other Oceanic books by Nordhoff and Hall which have been filmed include *Tuttles of Tahiti* (1942) and *The High Barbaree* (1947), neither of which caused much of a stir. *Tuttles*, however, is a stylish Charles Laughton movie that perfectly captures the carefree indolence of South Sea life earlier this century. In terms of box-office hits, the only success the team had, besides *Mutiny*, was the three-times filmed *Hurricane* (1937, 1974 and 1979). The remakes are pure cornball, but the 1937 version was very popular and made a huge star of Dorothy Lamour. Just as Lana Turner took to the sweater, Lamour and her sarong became inseparable screen buddies (no matter that in Polynesia they call it a pareu). After this, she was seldom portrayed anywhere other than the tropics, or in anything other than a wrap-around, with a huge flower in her hair. The film actually seems to contain few Polynesians, being shot in the studio, with only a little intercut footage of Tahiti. Lamour, of course, didn't look Polynesian, but her languid, sloe-eyed gaze and the obvious associations of her surname made her evocative of sexy South Seas glamour.

Today, more democratic casting standards and a more extensive use of location shooting has resulted in greater authenticity. *Rapa Nui* (1994) is an imaginative recreation of Easter Island history which uses such spectacular backdrops as the Orongo cliffs and the island's great crater. Furthermore, Polynesian star Jason Scott Lee was cast in the lead. The making of the film was also remarkable in providing employment for 90% of the island's workforce.

Looking as sultry as the weather, with a tatoo on the neck, Mel Gibson played the fourth movie Fletcher Christian in The Bounty, *1984*

The celebrated image of swaying grass skirts, rhythmic drums and soft guitars under the palms have made the islands a prime site for the musical. Even back in 1929, Ramon Navarro's part-talkie *The Pagan* had musical sequences (he plays, rather oddly, a singing Polynesian shopkeeper) which proved what a pleasant tenor voice the actor had. In general, the islands formed a cardboard backdrop against which various musical subjects could be paraded. In *Hawaiian Nights* (1939), the hero is a big-band conductor in Honolulu; *Hawaii Calls* (1939) features the singer of a cruise liner's orchestra; Dennis O'Keefe is a Papeete pianist in *Tahiti Honey* (1943); and another band leader crops up in *Tahiti Nights* (1945). At least *The Pagan Love Song* (1950) rang a few changes, with Howard Keel as an American teacher hotfooting it to Tahiti to take over his uncle's coconut plantation. This MGM musical also had the sense to lug its cameras across to Hawaii, and then, with an abundance of water around, exploit the aqua-choreographic talents of Esther Williams. The movie even had a hit song in the evocatively entitled 'The House of Singing Bamboo'. Some of these South Sea movie musicals, however, featured song titles as deliriously dreadful as the plots. 'The Cockeyed Mayor of Jaunakakai', 'Koni Plenty Hu-Hu' and 'I Left Her on the Beach at Waikiki' just about sum them up. Not that the plots and song titles of Presley's musicals were much better.

Elvis Presley's association with Hawaii began in 1961 and continued, off and on, into the early seventies. He first arrived on the islands to perform a memorial benefit concert for the lives lost in 1941 on the Japanese-sunk USS *Arizona*. His sojourn was then prolonged by the location shooting for *Blue Hawaii*, a movie which turned out to be Elvis's most successful film ever, if not his best. The plot, like so many of his movies, is thin enough to use as a string on which to hang scenery, songs and soirées. In this case, to include as much island scenery as possible, Elvis plays a tour guide whose parents own a pineapple plantation. The connection with tourism is significant. The new state of Hawaii had only joined the union a few years previously in 1959, so the Hawaiian Tourist Board was delighted to welcome Paramount Pictures and a star like Elvis Presley to the islands. And, indeed, the glamorous package did serve to promote the islands lavishly, helping open them up as a holiday destination, particularly for the North American mainland. The movie acted, in this sense, like a cunning travel brochure, with Elvis as our celebrity guide. Such famous locations as Waikiki Beach, Ala Moana Park, Lydgate Park and the Coco Palms Resort Hotel were used in the film — even Honolulu jail got a look in. Elvis also managed to create a fashion for the now ubiquitous Hawaiian shirt.

The important point was how comfortably he slipped into the languid pace of island life, appearing so relaxed and natural that his pleasure conveyed itself to his audiences. Whether performing a quite acceptable hula, goofing about in the lagoon, slurping pineapple, or bursting into song in an outrigger canoe, he made everything about island life seem ever-youthful, carefree fun. The location work on the lovely island of Kauai (earlier used for *South Pacific*) also gave the movie a visual splendour no studio trickery could have begun to capture. Elvis was so comfortable with Hawaii and the filming that he later joked about the 'Hawaiian Wedding Song' sequence: 'It seemed so real I thought I really married the chick!'

Making *Blue Hawaii*, and returning to the islands time and time again for vacations, proved to be amongst the happiest moments of his ultimately tragic life. He made two more movies there — *Girls! Girls! Girls!* (1962) and *Paradise Hawaiian Style* (1965) — with mixed results. The formula was definitely wearing thin. Presley's love affair with the fiftieth state, however, could not be eclipsed by the experience of these two mediocre vehicles. He gave his 'Kui Lee Cancer Drive' concert, and in 1973 came the historic 'Aloha from Hawaii via Satellite' concert, from the Honolulu International Center. In this way, Elvis brought the islands to his public, and gave them a more traditional, romantic image than the TV series of the period, 'Hawaii Five-0' — which was based mainly in downtown Honolulu. Even when not on the islands, Elvis was often photographed wearing the style of yachting cap he first sported in *Girls! Girls! Girls!*

There is one movie, though, which has evoked more South Sea dreaming than all of the rest put together. It speaks volumes that *South Pacific* (1958) ran in London's West End for a staggering four years and twenty-two weeks, qualifying as the longest continuous run in British cinema history. The story behind it takes us back to World War II.

On 7th December 1941, the Japanese attacked Pearl Harbor, then shortly after invaded Micronesia and Melanesia. Nauru, the Gilberts, Guam and New Guinea all succumbed, then the invaders headed into the Solomons, with Bougainville and Guadalcanal seeing the heaviest of the fighting. Nouméa, on the French island of New Caledonia, became the headquarters for the US forces, with other strategic bases further north in the New Hebrides (now Vanuatu). It was here, in the south-western Pacific, that the battle raged, with various islands in Polynesia (Tonga, Tahiti, Samoa, the Cooks and Bora Bora) being drawn in as supply bases.

Into this theatre of war — to a part of the world most people until then had only seen in the movies, or read about in books — came the thirty-six-year-old New York-born, short-sighted lieutenant James Michener. The irony is that this man, who came to be christened by the press 'Mr Pacific', almost never made it to the part of the world which made him famous. Michener is a Quaker, and as such came very close to registering as a conscientious objector.

Working as 'a kind of superclerk for the naval air forces', he was based on Espiritu Santo in the New Hebrides. Between spring 1944 and autumn 1945, he followed the action on forty-nine islands, travelling some 150,000 miles (241,400 kilometres) across the Pacific. For eight months, he followed the forces, inspecting ground installations, overseeing supplies, delivering messages and speaking to soldiers and natives. 'I usually got to the islands three days after the fighting was over,' he reported. 'It was like going to a Sunday picnic when I landed, and we just walked ashore.'

As publications officer for the Solomons, Michener was given his own quonset hut, a jeep, two men at his disposal and the use of various craft, with which he could travel from island to island. He had plenty of time to note the behaviour of his fellow officers in these alien conditions, as well as studying the islands, their people and folklore, and the European settlers. Never was there a better opportunity for observing the interaction between the previously isolated islanders and the awe-struck Westerners. Everything about these two sets of people was dissimilar — what they ate, what they thought, how they lived. Nevertheless, islanders and soldiers were drawn together by a mutual horror of war. It was also apparent that hosts and visitors had a mutual fascination with each other. The Americans were seduced by the spectacle of Oceania, even as they planned battle strategies and fought on the beaches. For their part, the islanders were pleasantly surprised by the equality with which they were treated by the servicemen, and startled to see black soldiers standing side by side with white. Things would clearly never be the same again from either perspective.

At Luganville, on Santo, over 100,000 US servicemen lived in a huge military base, some bizarre remnants of which still remain. (With typical South Pacific practicality, quonset huts have now been turned into houses, Marston matting from the airstrips has become fencing, and ammunition bunkers and gun emplacements have been transformed into copra and coffee-bean driers.)

While he was on Santo, Michener formed an officers' discussion group, and it was at these meetings that he was encouraged by friends to set down his experiences and thoughts on paper. One evening, returning from one of the sessions, he lit a lantern in his tin shack, ignited a mosquito bomb, and sat down at his typewriter to begin *Tales of the South Pacific*:

> *I wish I could tell you about the South Pacific. The way it actually was. The endless ocean. The infinite specks of coral we call islands. Coconut palms nodding gracefully towards the ocean. Reefs upon which waves broke into spray, and inner lagoons, lovely beyond description. I wish I could tell you about the sweating jungle, the full moon behind the volcanoes ... But whenever I start to talk about the South Pacific, people intervene.*

And what people they are — Nellie Forbush, Emile de Becque, Bloody Mary, Lt. Joe Cable, Liat and Luther Billis. All of them have walked out of the pages of the stories and into modern South Pacific myth. Some are based on actual people James met. Nellie, the twenty-two-year-old nurse from Arkansas with bobbed hair and gingham halter, derives from a navy nurse who was indeed married on a plantation. And the plantation owner de Becque, her sophisticated French lover, is based upon several planters Michener knew, but especially upon an Australian coast-watcher who operated in the Upper Solomons. Then there is the fifty-year-old round and raucous Tonkinese woman, teeth stained with betelnut juice, who sold shrunken heads — and love. Bloody Mary (who has a fast-food restaurant named after her in Vila, on Efate, was in part based was a real Tonkinese character who Michener had met on a plantation. In 1986, the author returned to the area for a CBS Television *60 Minutes* documentary, and found the other woman on whom he had modelled Bloody Mary was still alive. Aggie Grey of Western Samoa (who started the hotel named after her in Apia) died two years later in 1988. Everyone who watched the programme was as moved as Michener himself.

Once he was into his stride, between autumn 1944 and spring 1945, Michener worked on his manuscript day and night. He retired to the big empty warehouse of a cocoa plantation after watching the evening movie and, armed with a handful of mosquito bombs, he often typed on into the small hours. It is no wonder that he was moved to set Nellie's first date with Emile in such a location: 'A cocoa grove, in rainy weather, is a mournful and lovely place. In bright sunlight it is a hall of mirrors, and at dusk it has a quality of deep jungle quiet and mysteriousness that is equalled nowhere else in the tropics.'

After discharge, by the end of 1946, Michener had sold two chapters of his book to the *Saturday Evening Post*. By February 1947, Macmillan published *Tales of the South Pacific*, and a year later the Pulitzer Prize Committee awarded the book their honour. Michener had a winner on his hands, with its meld of realism and romance played out against lagoon and palm. His set of stories, which some commentators talk about as a novel, also brought him great critical acclaim. In fact, beside the huge, looser, doorstop-size novels he would later produce, it is still considered his finest work.

There were, of course, other authors, some of whom fought in the Pacific, who added to the relevant literature. There was Nordhoff and Hall's *The High Barbaree* (1945), Richard Nash's *Mister Roberts* (1946), Norman Mailer's *The Naked and the Dead* (1948), James Jones's *From Here to Eternity* (1951), Herman Wouk's *The 'Caine' Mutiny* (1951) and Eugene Burdick's *The Ninth Wave* (1956) and *The Blue of Capricorn* (1960). Yet only Michener, Burdick, and Nordhoff and Hall wove into their epics of war the sensual, savage beauty of the islands and their people. Michener's characters did not merely pass through the South Pacific, they interacted with its people; it touched off romantic dreams inside them and changed them for ever.

The book's mix of romance and drama made it the perfect material for a Broadway show. In 1948, Rodgers and Hammerstein approached Michener to turn some of the stories into a musical.

Burt Lancaster and Deborah Kerr wrestle amorously on a Hawaiian beach, innocent of the approaching drama of Pearl Harbor, in From Here to Eternity, *1953*

Michener delightedly agreed. The script, which concentrated on the stories 'Our Heroine', 'Fo' Dolla' and 'A Boar's Tooth' was, according to the author, 'finished without mussing an eyebrow on one of my characters'. While not himself undertaking any work on the adaptation, James did suggest 'Bali-Ha'i' for the title of the song which would sum up the story's spirit of haunting rapturous mystery.

After a sneak preview at Connecticut, Michener realised that he had made the correct decision: 'The whole tenor of the show is superb … The thing that impressed me was the warmth and right-heartedness of the whole damned thing.' He liked other things about it, too. The composers asked Michener if he would care to invest in the show. At the time, however, he and his wife were building a home in Bucks County and had no spare funds. Convinced that they had a smash hit, Rodgers and Hammerstein loaned James $4,500 to buy 6% of the property. He accepted, and the show went on to be the composers' most successful after *Oklahoma!* And, as if this were not enough, in 1958 it was turned into a hit movie musical, the most successful of all time, making *South Pacific* a very lucrative investment, which has provided Michener with a continuous income.

Locations for the movie were supplied by Hollywood's stand-by tropical island setting, Hawaii. This was very far from the Vanuatu setting of the original novel, but it did have the advantage of geographical convenience for the studios. Whereas Ensign Nellie Forbush should have been washing that man right out of her hair, say, on Santo's magnificent Champagne Beach, she did so instead on Kauai's splendid Lumahai Beach. This location, which is probably the most famous Hawaiian beach next to Waikiki, is now marked in all the tourist information as the setting most associated with the movie. And it is still an unspoilt setting for tropical reveries, with its lava rock, white sand, dazzling blue water and fringe of hala trees. Of course, one will not see Bali-h'ai across the sea in the distance — the inspiration for this is actually quite far from the movie's locations and something of a geographical amalgam. Bali-h'ai is modelled on the small island of Aoba, seen from Santo, with close-up details derived from the island of Mono, further north in the Treasuries.

The island locations, right from the opening shots of the movie, gave the drama, romance and the songs plenty of room to stretch out and breathe. The huge 70-mm Todd-AO screen helped convey the immensity of sky and sea, the size and grace of coconut palms. The extraordinary, unvarying brilliance of the sunlight was actually a problem for director Joshua Logan, who wanted to create different moods visually. For some people, however, the colour filters he eventually resorted to, and regretted afterwards, actually destroy any moods he had in mind.

Rodgers and Hammerstein were particularly attracted to the counterpointed love stories: the nurse and the French planter, and the lieutenant and the Tonkinese woman. In these twin romantic dramas, they had the themes of race and class which they had pursued elsewhere. The theme of island seduction was one which had preoccupied most South Sea writers. On these beautiful shores, so remote from home-grown values, young people lost their inhibitions. Guilt, however, could wreck a relationship, even a life, as Somerset Maugham never tired of pointing out in his Oceanic stories. This, then, was the backbone of the musical, and one of the highlights was when Cable sings to Nellie about what the folks back home would think of his island lover ('You've Got to be Carefully Taught').

Rodgers was initially confused as to how to compose the right kind of music for this part of the world. He asked Michener, 'When I score this music, do I have to use a wailing guitar?' The writer replied, 'In the part of the South Pacific I was in, I never heard such an instrument.' (Actually, the so-called Hawaiian guitar is really of Portuguese origin.) From believing that he would have to make heavy use of ukulele, xylophone and marimba, Rodgers was delighted with the news that 'in this part of the South Pacific there was no instrumental music of any kind' (other than percussive, that is). His only musical concession to the islands was a vaguely oriental use of harmonies for songs like 'Bali-Ha'i'. Indeed, the striking three-note motif which indicates this isle of dreams was used to open the show.

This vivid tale of characters seizing love while they can, in an unfamiliar paradise torn apart by war, has come to stand for everything the South Pacific offers — adventure, romance and spectacle. Not that it is Michener's last word on the subject. In 1949, he returned to the area for a series of articles for *Holiday Magazine*, and from his experiences was born *Return to Paradise*, another

An important meeting to sign contracts for the creation of the musical, South Pacific. From left to right: *producer Joshua Logan, composer Richard Rodgers, lyricist/librettist Oscar Hammerstein, star Mary Martin and original author James Michener*

best-seller. One of the stories, 'Mr Morgan', about a white man on a remote atoll, was turned into a 1953 film, with Gary Cooper. Shot on the Samoan island of Upolu, in the vicinity of a beach near Lefaga, the location has since become known as Return to Paradise Beach.

The islands of the Pacific were also responsible for Michener's prototype mega-novel *Hawaii* (1959). This huge, sprawling work — heroically undertaken on a manual typewriter in a tiny apartment in Waikiki — opens with Hawaii's emergence from the ocean, pursues the intertwined fates of various fictional families, and concludes with the election day of 1954. Certain Hawaiian groups complained that the book played fast and loose with island history, but none the less it became a mammoth best-seller. The film was released in 1966 but, even at 189 minutes, could only relay a fraction of Michener's narrative. Oddly enough, Norway stood in for some of the Hawaiian locations, and the whole thing was given a suitably heroic mould by the presence of Richard Harris's huge voice and shoulders. Hollywood came back for more, however, with *The Hawaiians* in 1970, utilizing the hallowed screen image of Charlton Heston to pump up the importance of an overlong sequel.

The South Pacific launched Michener's enormously successful career, just as its historically complex patterns of settlement forged his encyclopedic style. He has always acknowledged the central influence of Oceania upon his life. When once asked about the secret of his success, and what essential advice he would offer the tyro novelist, he replied half-seriously: 'Be sure your novel is read by Rodgers and Hammerstein.' But, just as Michener toasts the South Pacific, the islands have honoured him:

> Recently, I returned to Bora Bora on a big ocean liner, arriving at dawn. The islanders had learned by radio that I was returning to an island on which I had served as an American patron, and which I had later written about with affection, naming it repeatedly as the most beautiful island in the world. When we sailed into the perfect lagoon, some thirteen old-style war canoes laden with men, women, fruits and flowers came surprisingly to greet us. With a bullhorn, a chief cried, 'James Michener, we welcome you back to our island.' They had in the lead canoe a chair-throne and on it I rode into shore covered with more leis than my head could hold, and all that day I was taken about the island to one community after another that I had helped during the war. And when we sailed at dusk, the shore was crowded with natives there to bid me farewell … and the waves were filled with flowers.

The essence of South Seas' romance: hick navy nurse Nellie Forbush (Mitzi Gaynor) meets suave French plantation owner Emile de Becque (Rossano Brazzi) in South Pacific

At the climax of Blue Hawaii, *Elvis marries the half-Polynesian heroine Maile (Joan Blackman),*
and performs the 'Hawaiian Wedding Song'. He was so carried away by the island atmosphere that he reported,
'It seemed so real I thought I really married the chick'

Lucy Irvine on Tuin Island searching for shells in the lagoon

CHAPTER EIGHT

AN

ISLAND APART

THE ONCE-SLEEPY islands of the South Pacific have been dragged kicking into the twentieth century. The pressures of tourism and the problems of colonialism have taken their toll on certain parts of the region. Even so, alongside the colonist and the ever-present package tourist, Oceania has continued to attract the more adventurous, independent seeker of utopia. Within these ranks, there is a certain amount of cynicism and disillusionment among the visiting writers. Nothing, however, has deterred a steady stream of intrepid Europeans pursuing the genuine South Sea experience on the region's multitude of uninhabited islands. Whether as comfortable privately-owned sanctuaries, or as rudimentary proving grounds for romantic self-survivalists, the islands today are as popular as they have ever been.

As dissimilar as they may appear to be at first, the private owner and the latterday Crusoe are brothers under the skin. No matter that the private owner often transforms an isolated paradise into a luxury mini-resort for the well-heeled dreamer. Sometimes such measures prove inevitable in order to finance a lifestyle that has no connection with mainland routine, or to help maintain the island's delicate ecological balance on a day-to-day basis. The important factor in the equation is the fantasy of an island apart, a place to live a simpler life. Neither the private owner nor those who are Crusoe-fixated actually manage to 'go native', however. While owners combine a few too many mainland comforts with island traditions, the Crusoes attempt a challenge which the average islander finds risibly unrealistic.

As mentioned before, one of the most famous examples of a twentieth-century personality seeking escape in the South Pacific is that of Marlon Brando. He came to Tahiti in 1962 to make the MGM version of *Mutiny on the Bounty*. Falling in love with his Tahitian leading lady, Tarita Teriipia, also seemed to involve an affair with the islands themselves. By 1963, after much toing and froing between Los Angeles and Tahiti, he decided to make a permanent home for himself and Tarita in the South Seas. The demands of his career, not to mention his continuing marriage to small-time Mexican actress Movita Castenada, were putting a strain upon their relationship. He envisaged the islands as a healthy environment in which to bring up the children he would have with Tarita. Besides which, Brando felt that the islands would solve the problem of his increasing need for privacy.

One of the places he was particularly interested in purchasing was the uninhabited coral atoll of Tetiaroa, a beautiful necklace of tiny islands 25 miles (40 kilometres) north of Tahiti. Once the playground of Tahitian aristocracy, in 1904 it was presented to a British dentist in repayment for all the royal Tahitian teeth he had filled. By the early sixties, the dentist's granddaughter had put the property on the market, and Brando went to view it.

His introduction to the atoll proves the point about the private owner's special relationship with their island. To begin with, Brando rejected a motorboat as his mode of transport in favour of a traditional rowing boat manned by four Tahitians. Already, it was no ordinary guided tour by an estate agent but an adventure in itself. The adventure went beyond his wildest dreams, however. The boat was torn apart in one of the dangerous passages through the reef, and all those aboard were forced to swim to the nearest isle. With no means of communication, they were trapped as castaways on the atoll for two days, existing on coconuts and native beans.

Brando was profoundly moved by the experience. Something of a moody outsider, he seemed to thrive on the feeling of total isolation, risk and the challenge of self-survival. It had an almost purifying effect upon him. He bought the island as a place to find himself again, as an antidote to the fatuous bustle and brittle sophistication of Los Angeles.

Until the early seventies, Tetiaroa was Brando's private retreat to a simpler life. He lived in a thatched hut on the beach of Tiaraunu, the largest island, with only palm fronds across the windows, to catch the breezes. He wandered along the sands in a pareu, planning how to improve his haven. One of these was the erection of some windmills for grinding corn, to be driven by the trade winds. He developed a coconut plantation, improved the conditions of the bird sanctuary on Tahuna Iti isle, and employed Tahitians to make canoes and undertake weaving, in the encouragement of traditional crafts.

Slowly but surely, however, financial reality reared its ugly head. Replanting trees, rebuilding huts lost in storms and the general upkeep of the atoll was costly. On top of this, he began to think in terms of Tetiaroa as a source of income for Tarita and their children. At last, it was decided to construct a native-style hotel complex on Tiaraunu. From islands beyond the atoll, materials were ferried in through the treacherous reef — coral, pandanus, kahaiha wood, palm trunks and leaves. In

1968, an airstrip was laid on the island and, by 1973, the complex was completed. By the late seventies, the commercial enterprise was a going concern.

By then, Brando had shifted his base elsewhere in the atoll. From time to time, between movies, he could be seen by visitors stalking about on the smaller islands, dressed eccentrically in a flowing mumu and huge straw hat. The press began to refer to Tetiaroa as 'Brando's fat farm', as he frequently went there to recover from uncontrollable eating binges. The pressures of his demanding career and complex love life were taking their toll. None the less, he was still optimistic enough about Tetiaroa to talk to the University of French Polynesia about setting up courses to study the history and ecology of his atoll.

In the end, it was Nature which stepped in to sour Brando's relationship with his island — his longest-lasting love affair. In 1982, a terrible cyclone devastated Tetiaroa, ripping up and flinging about many buildings and trees. Brando was profoundly disillusioned. His utopian retreat had been violated. His visits there grew fewer and farther between, and his communication with Tarita and the South Seas became only casual.

Richard Evanson, another lost soul hankering after the simpler life, found himself in Fiji in 1972. Amongst his various careers, he had made a small fortune with a cable TV business in his native Seattle. One divorce later, deeply dispirited, he began to see his whole way of living as devoid of meaning and took off to explore the world. At a bar counter in Suva, capital of the big island of Viti Levu, he expressed the wish to have his own slice of this friendly, slow-paced paradise. The man on the next stool told him about Turtle Island (also known as Nanuya Levu), in the Yasawa Group, 50 miles (80 kilometres) north of Viti Levu. It was beautiful, and had been unoccupied for twenty-three years.

Having stepped upon the perfect beach of Turtle Island, there was no going back for Evanson. He purchased the island for $300,000 and set himself up in a shack by the side of the lagoon. His only luxury was a dilapidated, generator-run refrigerator in which he cooled several six-packs of beer. He had been alone for all of 20 minutes when Joe Naisali, a teenager from a neighbouring island, paddled over to welcome him. Evanson believes that the Fijians are, 'The most lovely, warm, wonderful, caring people in the world,' and Joe stayed on to become his Man Friday.

Evanson settled down to a blissfully unadorned lifestyle. He fished, planted vegetables and trees, and built a house for a mere $200. As with Brando, he considers his simpler, early days upon the island as a purifying experience for body and soul. Such times may well have continued, but for the intervention of fate — in the shape of Columbia Pictures. In 1978, the studio wanted to hire the island to remake *The Blue Lagoon* — the 1948 Jean Simmons version was also made there. They offered $250,000, as well as undertaking to make certain civilizing improvements to the real estate, which the owner was welcome to retain.

At the time, Evanson was not growing bored so much as a little lonely. He had befriended American actor Raymond Burr, of 'Ironside' fame, who had purchased the Fijian island of Naitamba. Burr, however, was based in Hollywood, so his company could not be relied upon. Columbia's offer, therefore, was not one he could refuse. Headed by Brooke Shields, the movie's nymphet Girl Friday, an eighty-strong production team took over the island, constructing several local-style cottages ('bures'), the major part of what is now the main lodge, and a dock. There is an anecdote, which Evanson likes to relate, that when the team were given a short vacation from the filming, most of them chose to stay on the island.

From this invasion was born the idea of Turtle Island Resort. Evanson had been awakened, as it were, from his big sleep as Crusoe. He loved the Fijians — he had even married one or two — but he could not shake off his craving for Western company. Yet with just twenty-eight guests at a time, and fifty-five full-time staff, the island still retains a languorous pace and sense of privacy — from the 400-foot (122-metre) peak of Mount Ford to the turquoise waters of the aptly-named Blue Lagoon.

Just as Brando used to, Evanson has chosen to improve the ecology of his world apart. Four of his full-time staff are dedicated to planting trees. When he arrived, the island was only 10% wooded, but later this increased to an impressive 50%. By planting trees, both decorative (Plumeria) and useful (Norfolk Pine), he has created a modified, more humid rain forest environment. His goal is to shade the 10 miles (16 kilometres) of trail around the island with overhanging vegetation. Some people take their dreams seriously.

The dock of Pitcairn Island, turn of the century, where descendants of the Bounty *mutineers still live. The Pitcairn Islanders are an example of one of the most successful, large-scale attempts at playing Crusoe*

Like Brando, the late Malcolm Forbes did not make his South Sea island a permanent residence — at least while he was alive. After all, Mr Forbes had a few other properties on hand — an estate in Bali, a palace in Morocco, a Normandy chateau, a Wren-designed London mansion, and a family estate in New Jersey. This would seem to bear out the rumour that Forbes was impressed by the fact that King Tutankhamun made his mark upon history more by the wealth he had accumulated than by what he did for Egypt.

Multi-millionaire, self-styled 'Capitalist Tool' and extravagant showman, Forbes was nevertheless like any other man with a fantasy when it came to his Fijian island of Laucala, off Vanua Levu. One of those fortunate enough to be able to buy dreams, Forbes had fulfilled his romantic fantasies about the near-mythical island of Bali-h'ai. When he first saw Laucala in 1972, he was stunned by the fact that it 'looked more like Bali-h'ai than the cover of the sheet music'. Like Michener's legendary island, though, Laucala was not uninhabited. Around 300 people lived there.

Forbes bought his Bali-h'ai for a million dollars, complete with native extras. Unlike the early days of Brando and Evanson, however, Forbes was never interested in roughing it and returning to a state of blissful simplicity. Instead, he went for instant development. Native-style bures were built along the beach for paying guests, and an impressive ranch, the Plantation House, was constructed on a hill for family and friends. Not taking his responsibilities lightly, he also built for the Laucalans new bungalows, a repair workshop, a general store, a school, a church and a wharf. To help provide employment all round, he also laid an airstrip, shuttling guests to and fro in the island's own plane, drily christened *Capitalist Tool Too*.

At what point does business cancel out 'paradise'? By admitting that 'our guests have turned out to be a better cash crop than copra' and that he had dragged the Laucalans 'from coconuts to credit cards, all in one generation', Forbes may seem to be contradicting the utopian ethic. Yet Brando, Evanson and Forbes brought improvements to their three islands, which continue to thrive in a state of languid contentment. It is the case with most of the tiny private islands of the South Seas, that their development has been far more sensitively tackled than the careless modernisation of many of the main islands.

As for Forbes the man, he seems to be remembered primarily for the prestigious *Forbes Magazine* empire, his penchant for hot-air ballooning and Fabergé eggs, and the fact that he must be the only millionaire to have had an adoring contingent of Hell's Angels turn up to his funeral. (He rode a Harley-Davidson up to the end of his life.) Yet perhaps the most telling personal detail — the equivalent, perhaps, of discovering the significance of Citizen Kane's sled *Rosebud* — is the fact that when Forbes died in 1990, he was not buried on his 40-acre (16-hectare) family estate in New Jersey, as one would have assumed. At his request, his ashes were interred instead on Laucala. With an endearing whimsicality, he chose to pass eternity on Bali-h'ai.

To some, a refrigerator in which to chill your vintage champagne, not to mention air-conditioning to cool yourself, are anathema to the true ambience of South Sea island life. To those who would find the islands of Brando, Evanson and Forbes an artificial paradise, the simpler joys of warm coconut water, fish from the lagoon grilled over a fire, and a palm-frond shelter, are much more acceptable. The archetype for such an austere island life is, of course, Robinson Crusoe — or, to be more exact, his real-life model, Alexander Selkirk.

On 15th June 1708, two ships sailed from Bristol. They were the *Duke*, of 300 tons, under the command of Captain Woodes Rogers, and the *Duchess*, of 270 tons. Both ships were commissioned by the Lord High Admiral to cruise the Pacific coasts of South America and Mexico against England's enemies, the French and the Spanish. On 1st February 1709, they came across the island of Juan Fernández, off Chile, where they hove to for the night. When, after dark, they saw the light of a fire on the shore, they decided to investigate the next day, to search for pirates or an enemy garrison.

What they found instead was 'one poor naked man', named Alexander Selkirk (1676–1721). In May 1703, this Scotsman from Fife had sailed to the South Seas as master of the 96-ton *Cinque-ports*, under Captain Dampier. After a difference with his commander in September 1704, Selkirk had agreed to be put ashore for a time at Juan Fernández. Whatever went wrong, however, he found himself alone there until his rescue by Rogers almost five years later. His tale was recorded by the captain.

It seems that for Selkirk the first eight months were the worst, in which he was overcome with melancholy at the thought of dying a forgotten and lonely old man (in reality, there never was any Man, or even Girl Friday). Fortunately, his terror was offset by the sheer necessity to survive. He built two huts of pimento-tree wood, grass and goat skin, living in one and using the other as a larder. He lived mainly on crayfish, wild goat, and cabbages and turnips planted by Dampier on a previous trip. The island was overrun with rats and cats, who had abandoned various ships, but by befriending the former, he kept the latter at bay. Selkirk had even managed to avoid landing parties from enemy ships by smartly shinning up the nearest tree.

Although Selkirk did not have a refrigerator or air-conditioning, rather like the guest celebrities of the enduring British radio show 'Desert Island Discs', he had been allowed to select certain personal items to make life as a castaway that little bit more agreeable. 'He had with him,' wrote Captain Rogers, 'his clothes and bedding, with a firelock, some powder, bullets, and tobacco, a hatchet, a knife, a kettle, a Bible, some practical pieces, and his mathematical instruments and books.'

If this seems a little disappointing to self-survival purists, it must be remembered that it was Selkirk's back-to-the-wall resourcefulness and ultimate conquest over loneliness which are the all-important keys to survival under any circumstances. It is against this casebook that we must measure all aspirations to be a latterday Crusoe.

'Crusoeism' is a fantasy which seems deeply embedded in human nature. The lure of the desert island is particularly strong today, in an era of high-pressure lifestyles, when technology has intruded into almost every corner of our day-to-day affairs. What would it actually be like to be thrown back upon one's own resources, to try to go back, as far as possible, to nature? And where better to take the test than those isolated flecks of land adrift in the immense Pacific Ocean?

Even in the second half of the 1800s, Papeete, Tahiti, was becoming developed and Westernized. Europeans fleeing to the South Seas to seek an island apart found they had to search the remotest regions

One of the problems with Crusoeism is Girl Friday. It appears significant that most of those who engage in this activity are single men looking for a lot more than palms and peace. And it never seems to work. Just as such Pacific desert islanders as Gerald Kingsland, Gary Hadfield and Martin Popplewell are ill at ease with civilization, so they also seem to have difficulties forging sexual relationships, even under the circumstances of isolation. The most famous of these three is Kingsland, though mainly because of the book written by his one-time island partner, Lucy Irvine.

In 1978, Kingsland gave up growing grapes in Italy, possessed by the spirit of Alexander Selkirk. Having once been in the British armed forces, he determined to return to a life of adventure. His initial attempt, which was a complete fiasco, was on Cocos Island, north of the Galapagos Islands. It proved to be shark and mosquito-infested, and crawling with unfriendly Costa Rican police. In 1980, he went straight for Selkirk's own island, Juan Fernández. He arrived to discover that it now had an aerodrome, a small settlement and a great many sheep. When the much younger Girl Friday, Ann Conroy, arrived fresh from his appealing British newspaper advertisement, she added insult to injury by refusing to respond to his romantic overtures.

Kingsland's most favourable effort at genuine Crusoeism came a year later when he settled on the uninhabited island of Tuin, in the Torres Strait, between Australia and Papua New Guinea. This time he advertised for an island bride, and found the very personable Ms Irvine. They aimed at lasting out a year, but Nature conspired pitilessly. It was not, anyway, a pretty island, being an unglamorous blend of rocks, mangroves and bush. There was only a small creek, scant rainfall, little fruit and several crocodiles. Tuin was not user-friendly, and neither was Lucy, who made sex a weapon for survival. Both grew quite ill, and the 1987 film version, *Castaway*, made it all seem far more romantic than it actually was. Lucy, at least, got something out of it — a best-selling book and a movie spin-off.

Englishman Martin Popplewell, nineteen-year-old son of a Cambridge business consultant, was inspired to flee from the twentieth century when he first saw the film *The Blue Lagoon* in 1985. His planning included meeting and talking to the Desert Island Queen, Lucy Irvine. It was not until 1989, however, that he found his island — tiny, uninhabited Sorenleng, in the Ulithi atoll of Micronesia. Here he planned to stay, as long as was possible, with his college friend Rachel Stevens who, from the outset, stipulated a no-sex rule. The island was beautiful, though little more than coconut palms and beach.

Rachel, however, was a strict vegetarian, and while Martin tucked healthily into the island's colony of coconut crabs, there was no protein for her to keep up her strength. Besides this set-back, Martin was starry-eyed enough to crave the love which the perfect couple in his favourite movie had enjoyed. 'I slept beneath a moon and stars so bright I could have read a book by them,' he wrote plaintively in his diary. 'It is times like this that I do wish we were lovers.' But they remained, in a sad sense, strangers in paradise.

The rift grew wider when Martin became more reliant upon such 'civilized' emergency rations as rice and beans, while Rachel struggled on with whatever the island offered. She came from the purist school of self-survival, having evidently not consulted the life of Selkirk. She could not even bear Martin to use nails to build a shelter, and refused point blank to listen to his cassette player.

He once took pity on her growing weakness, caused by the self-inflicted diet, and helped her swim to a neighbouring island to gather a hoard of breadfruit nuts. Regretfully, after only a few months, Rachel left Sorenleng. She loved the island's physical beauty and peacefulness, but the strictures of her diet were rendering her constantly ill. Martin was sadly forced to follow, his dream never fully realized.

Thirty-four-year-old Gary Hadfield, an ex-soldier from Oldham, Lancashire, in the north of England, had no such dreams of paradise — which was the main drawback of his exploit. Gary was a loner who saw his South Sea adventure as an extension of his military survival courses and, hopefully, a chance to attract a mate. In 1990, he set up an open-ended arrangement with the authorities to stay on the desert island of Tatongros, in the Carolines. Gary's first setback was when he approached his various female pen-pals, but failed to pull a Girl Friday.

The jungle terrain of his little island included giant red ants and mosquitoes, so that he was forced to sweat away the hours in a tracksuit for protection. The island was only half a mile long, and he could walk around it in an hour. Each day seemed to drag by, filled with picking coconuts and papaya, fishing and gathering wood. It was loneliness which broke his spirit after only two months, and drove him back to his terraced redbrick house.

Marlon Brando and Tarita Teriipia pose against Moorea on the horizon, and maybe discuss seeing an estate agent about buying an island. Mutiny on the Bounty, *1962*

The atoll of Tetiaroa, which became Brando's personal bolt-hole in 1963

Richard Evanson takes it easy in the shade of some palms on his beautiful Fijian retreat of Turtle Island

The 'Welsh Family Williams' cool off in their personal lagoon on Maina Island, Aitutaki Atoll, in the Cooks

There is one South Pacific Crusoe who has plunged all the others — even Selkirk himself — into the shade. In his late fifties, New-Zealand born Tom Neale lived alone on Anchorage Island, in the atoll of Suvorov in the Cooks, for three spells, between 1952–54, 1960–63 and 1967–77. A gentle, unpretentious, though wholly obsessed man, he spent the best part of six years in almost complete solitude, and would have continued to do so quite happily had age and ill health not curbed his obsession. He chose this way of living not to prove himself to anyone, and not with any great role model in mind, but simply because it seemed to him to be the most natural and satisfying mode of existence. 'I chose to live in the Pacific islands,' he wrote, 'because life there moves at the sort of pace which you feel God must have had in mind originally when He made the sun to keep us warm and provided the fruits of the earth for the taking.'

Whereas all our Crusoes so far have viewed sex as part and parcel of their private utopias, to Neale it was anathema. How could you expect two separate personalities to co-exist in such cramped physical conditions for an open-ended period of time? Of course, there would be certain advantages, such as a second person in case of any accidents. And then there was the not inconsiderable matter of erotic diversion to help pass the time pleasurably. To many a Crusoe, it would seem a shame to waste all that moonlight. However, Tom was adamant, even turning down several offers from Rarotongan women on his way to Anchorage. Maybe he should have renamed his island Anchorite.

Maybe here we have one of the key characteristics of the successful castaway: the loner, or hermit, mentality. After all, Selkirk himself, the prototype, asked to be left alone on Juan Fernández fully aware that the unforeseen could leave him stranded. Although the experiments of Kingsland, Hadfield and Popplewell proved interesting in themselves, it could be that their overall frustrations as self-survivalists sprang from having the initial scenario all wrong.

Tom Neale cheated on only one count. The island had upon it a quite serviceable hut built originally as a coastguard's lookout in World War II. (Visiting sailors to the island still keep the hut standing and in good repair, in memory of the man who has become an almost mythical figure of the modern Pacific.) Tom can be forgiven this luxury, though, in view of his almost wholly successful physical and psychological adaptation to his new environment. Very small islands fail to supply all the basics of a healthy and varied diet, and Neale was forced from the start to eliminate Anchorage's populations of wild pigs and land crabs, as they competed too aggressively with him for what food the island offered. He then grew vegetables on the fertile ground in the centre of the island, and raised chickens from the resident wild flock.

Routine became essential, significant and satisfying: making coffee in the morning, feeding the chickens, weeding the vegetable patch, an afternoon siesta, boiling the sheets once a week, fishing, building a fire in the evening to cook upon and another to sit beside on the beach. Intervals from the routine were like holidays. He would venture across the huge inner lagoon of the atoll to visit an islet, or 'motu', opposite. With Crusoe as a model, he even built himself a smaller secondary residence on this motu, a hut made of pandanus wood and thatching.

All was not, however, smooth sailing. Tom had three serious scrapes with death — once from fever, once when a storm tossed him from his canoe into the lagoon and once when a shark came too close. He was rescued from his fever, the worst of these tribulations, by the timely arrival of a visiting yachtie. Other casual visitors were not really welcome, and solitude seemed a small price to pay for the luxury of his existence.

When he left Anchorage, it was like tearing himself away from a lover. But, by 1977, he was suffering from cancer, and returned to Rarotonga. 'I realised I was getting on, and the prospect of a lonely death did not particularly appeal to me ... the time had come to wake up from an exquisite dream before it turned into a nightmare.' Another was that his desert island was no longer quite so deserted. A party of pearl divers from Manihiki descended on his privacy for a couple of months each year, being far too lively and intrusive for the place to seem like his own any more.

He died in a hospital on Rarotonga and was buried, ironically, opposite the noisy airport. In his last days, his mind often drifted back to his island, especially his favourite time of the day — watching the sunset, with his cat on his lap and a mug of tea in his hand, in total and sublime contentment. He concludes his book, *An Island to Oneself*, with the words: 'I have a wealth of memories that no man can take away from me.'

Tom Neale's account of his adventure worked its magic on another man who suffered from island madness. In his early forties, Welshman Tony Williams, a school caretaker, was already obsessed with the exploits of Captain Bligh in Oceania, and the near-legendary adventures of Tom Neale finally decided him. From his dreary council house in West Cross, Swansea, Tony fantasized in time-honoured fashion: 'I thought all the time about getting away to a place of warm sand, blue skies and coconuts dropping softly from the trees to the sound of twanging guitars.' His friends and relatives called him 'Walter Mitty', but was it 'crazy to want to go further than the shops'?

Having at last convinced his own wife and three young children, he sought permission from the government of the Cook Islands. In the early 1990s, scraping together the funds, Tony and his wife Cath made a trial visit prior to taking their children. Arriving, like Neale, on the main Cook island of Rarotonga, he was immediately struck by 'the smell of fruit and flowers and the warmth of the air, so sensuous on the skin'. The desert island choice was that of Takutea, north-west of Rarotonga. Larger than they had imagined, it was not very lush, being greatly exposed to the fierce tropical sun. They fished, knocked down coconuts to eat and drink from, and communicated with each other in a way they had not done since the early days of their relationship.

The two-month trial having proved a success, they returned to Wales and planned the next leg of their adventure. Giving the rights for their story to the *Daily Mirror* newspaper, they were sponsored to return to the Cooks, where they settled on Maina, in the Aitutaki atoll. Maina was smaller than Takutea, but greener and with a more elevated central section. A wild flock of chickens lived on this little isle, though they tasted overpoweringly of crab when trapped and cooked. The family adapted well, becoming healthier, stronger and slowing down to a sedate, dreamy pace. One unforeseen personal problem was that Tony's sex drive reached new heights — he blamed the

Tom Neale sits contentedly removing the flesh from coconuts to cook with fish. In the background is a boat he built himself

coconuts — at the same time as the couple had lost much of their privacy.

Having finally granted the *Mirror* its interviews, after a couple of months Tony was ready to move on to an even remoter isle. He chose Primrose, in the Palmerston atoll, and at last he found his own personal paradise. Cath, however, panicked and felt 'trapped'. On a mat of palm fronds, Tony meditated on the small beach for hours, staring out across the expansive azure lagoon. Not even a fierce storm, and the discovery of a colony of huge lizards, could put him off the peace and beauty of Primrose. As with Neale, however, sickness rudely awoke Tony from his reverie. Despite the luxury of having company on hand to help out, the problem of a fever urgently needed proper medical attention.

This variation on the Swiss Family Robinson — the Welsh Family Williams — is unique in the history of Crusoeism. Their six months on three uninhabited islands of the South Pacific is a wonderful example of one man's determination and the extraordinary adaptability of an average family.

◆ ◆ ◆

It says much that, for well over 200 years, since the South Pacific was first properly discovered, outsiders have been unable to stop dreaming of it. Still popularly seen as representing heaven on earth, before it is too late, these lovely islands must be preserved — for their own uniqueness, as well as for the powerful charm they have cast over so many. As Stevenson put it on his first Pacific landfall: 'The first experience can never be repeated. The first love, the first sunrise, the first South Sea island, are memories apart and touched by a virginity of sense.'

PICTURE CREDITS

SELECT BIBLIOGRAPHY

Louis Becke, *Pacific Tales*, KPI, London and New York, 1987.

Paul L. Briand Jr, *The Nordhoff–Hall Story: In Search of Paradise*, Mutual Publishing, Honolulu, 1987.

Jacques Brosse, *Great Voyages of Discovery: Circumnavigators and Scientists, 1764–1843*, Facts on File Publications, New York and Oxford, 1983.

Robert Dean Frisbie, *The Book of Puka-Puka*, Century, New York, 1928.

Paul Gauguin, *Noa Noa: The Tahitian Journal*, Dover, New York, 1985.

Arthur Grimble, *A Pattern of Islands*, John Murray, London, 1952.

A. Grove Day, *Mad About Islands: Novelists of a Vanished Pacific*, Mutual Publishing, Honolulu, 1987.

John La Farge, *An American Artist in the South Seas*, KPI, London and New York, 1987.

Jack London, *The Cruise of the Snark: A Pacific Voyage*, KPI, London and New York, 1986.

Pierre Loti, *The Marriage of Loti*, KPI, London and New York, 1986.

W. Somerset Maugham, *The Trembling of a Leaf*, Heinemann, London, 1953.

Margaret Mead, *Coming of Age in Samoa*, William Morrow & Co. Inc., New York, 1928.

James A. Michener, *Tales of the South Seas*, Corgi, 1987.

Alan Moorhead, *The Fatal Impact: An Account of the Invasion of the South Pacific, 1767–1840*, Hamish Hamilton, London, 1966.

Tom Neale, *An Island to Oneself: The Story of Six Years on a Desert Island*, Collins, London, 1966.

Robert Louis Stevenson, *Island Nights' Entertainment*, Hogarth Press, London, 1987. *Robert Louis Stevenson in the South Seas*, KPI, London and New York, 1987.

Paul Theroux, *The Happy Isles of Oceania: Paddling in the Pacific*, Hamish Hamilton, 1992.

INDEX

Italic numbers indicate illustrations

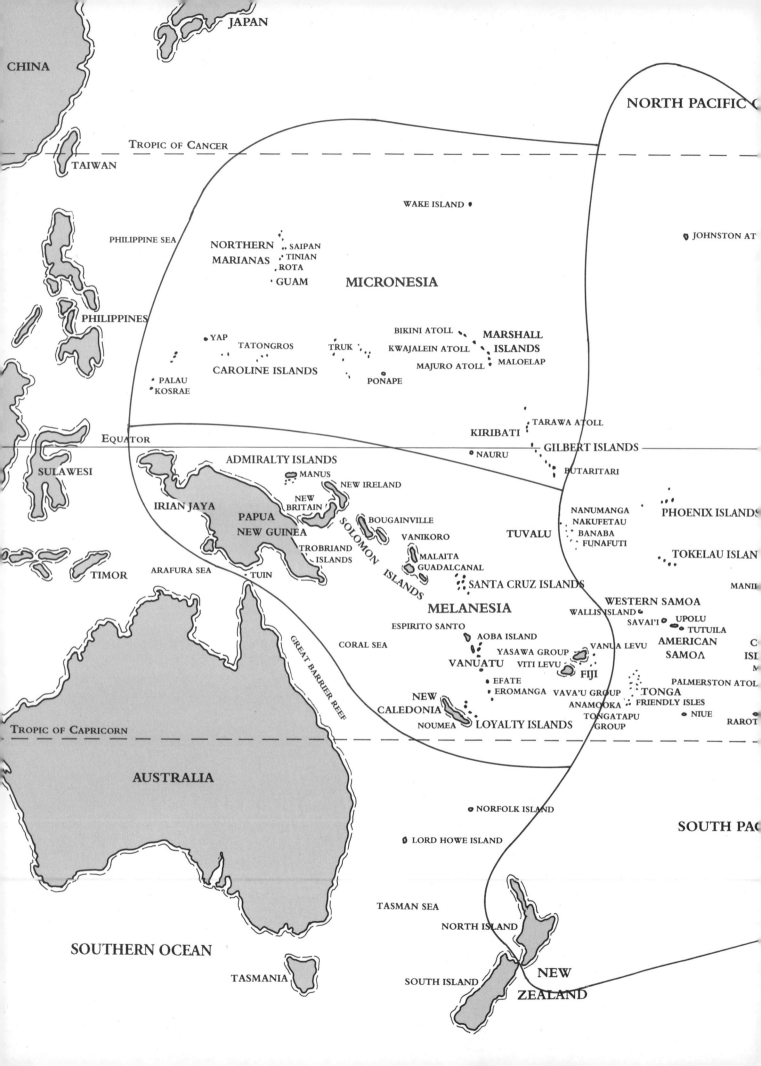